MURDER
AT CITY HALL

MURDER
AT CITY HALL

EDWARD I. KOCH
With Herbert Resnicow

KENSINGTON BOOKS

KENSINGTON BOOKS are published by

Kensington Publishing Corp.
850 Third Avenue
New York, NY 10022

Library of Congress Card Catalog Number: 95-076012
ISBN 0-8217-5087-9

First Printing: October, 1995

Printed in the United States of America

Dear Reader:

Being mayor of the City of New York, as I was from 1978 to 1989, has to be one of the most interesting jobs in this country. It is different from being the president or the governor, important as these positions are.

I think of my tenure as mayor as the most important time of my life—the apex of my professional career—and I'm glad and proud I experienced what only 107 people have experienced since New Amsterdam became New York City.

I have a fertile imagination that is still with me and, occasionally, I like to think about what life would be like if I could be mayor forever, head of the capital of the world, solving the city's problems and becoming more popular with the passage of each year, even more popular than the great Fiorello La Guardia.

While I was mayor, and since leaving office, I've written six books. I love to write, so I decided to create a fictional Ed Koch who could be mayor of New York forever in a series of mysteries. In these stories there will be tough fights against strong opponents and even against friends and colleagues. I'll be able to travel and to enjoy everything that makes New York great, to dine at the finest restaurants or to grab a hot dog from a street vendor, and occasionally turn amateur detective to help out a friend or colleague.

In these mysteries I'll have one unbreakable rule: the fictional characters I create will not be reminiscent of any of the many people with whom I came in contact when I was mayor. If at any time you, the reader, or any other person thinks that you see yourself depicted in these stories, it is because you have an active imagination. Believe me, you are *not* in my book.

In my books the bad guys are punished and the good guys, men and women, are rewarded, and that's the part of the fantasy I like best.

I have joined forces with Herb Resnicow, whose fertile mind can conjure up the plots of the criminals as mine moves to uncover those plots and catch the crooks.

Edward I. Koch

MURDER
AT CITY HALL

ONE

Of all the powers that the mayor of New York can exercise, one of the least used has to be the authority to perform marriages. Speaking for myself, I can only recall presiding at one such ceremony in the wedding chapel at City Hall. And with good reason. For that occasion led to murder . . .

Thursday morning started as usual with the limo arriving at 7:15 A.M. to transport me from Gracie Mansion to City Hall. Of course, I wasn't alone—I was accompanied, as always, by the Gang of Five, the NYPD detective sergeants who make up my bodyguard detail. Two men rode in the lead car, the other three in my limousine.

At that early hour, it's no more than a twenty-minute drive downtown, and it gives me a chance to look at the streets of Manhattan.

"Great day, isn't it?" Charley Deacon, my senior bodyguard, asked as the driver turned off East Eighty-sixth Street and headed down Fifth Avenue. Charley, a burly black man with distinguished-looking gray hair, lives in St. Albans, Queens. There's no one in New York I'd rather have guarding my body, even if I don't always agree with him.

This time, though, I did. "It *is* a great day." I gestured out the window at the wide avenue that seemed to gleam in the morning sunlight. "Will you look at that?"

"Supposed to get up into the eighties this afternoon. Feels more like July than April, doesn't it?"

"Nah, Charley, April in New York is always beautiful."

He chuckled. "To you, Mayor, New York is beautiful any time of year."

"Can't argue with that." I pressed the button to roll down my window, stuck my head out a little, and took a deep breath of fresh spring air as the limo slowed for a red light.

To our left was a row of majestic co-op buildings, each one fronted by an impeccably uniformed doorman. To our right, Central Park sprawled beyond a low stone wall. The sidewalk that ran alongside the park was dotted with joggers and stroller-pushing nannies and briefcase-toting office workers headed down to midtown.

One of them, a youngish man who had on pristine white Nikes with a charcoal Brooks Brothers suit, glanced my way and did a double take. I saw him nudge the woman he was with, a pretty brunette who wore black Reeboks with her conservative black dress and had an enormous black leather bag slung over her shoulder.

I could feel Charley grow slightly tense beside me. The two guys in the front seat, Paul Hurley and Lou Sabatino, glanced over their shoulders and then out the window at the two spectators. It's good to know my guards are always alert to possible danger—not that these pedestrian commuters could present any kind of threat. Still, as Charley would say, you never know.

I saw the man mouth the words, *it's the mayor* at the woman before he grinned and waved at me and shouted, "Hey, Ed! What's up?"

"How'm I doin'?" I called.

He responded with a prompt thumbs-up.

"That's what I like to hear," I commented to Charley, who nodded.

He was listening to the radio, which he always keeps very low so he won't disturb me. If anything comes on that I should know before I get to City Hall, he turns the volume up.

The light turned green and the limo moved forward. I settled back against the seat and let the warm breeze blow over me. In the park, the plane trees, the maples, and the ginkgoes were beginning to show green. Squirrels were chasing each other, and a couple of pigeons, along with two seagulls, were fighting over scraps of hot dogs and soft pretzels at the edge of the sidewalk.

"Anything interesting to report?" I asked Charley as we left Central Park behind. We were passing the Plaza on the right. The grand old hotel was surrounded as always by an impressive bustle of scurrying businesspeople and gawking, early-rising tourists, pushing through the wide main entrance doors or getting into and out of taxis in front.

"Traffic's heavy, with no major accidents," Charley told me. "The buses are still traveling in packs, and there's trouble on the uptown Number 1 train."

"What kind of trouble?" I had often taken that subway line back when I lived full-time in my three-room apartment on Washington Place in Greenwich Village.

"Work train broke down in the tunnel just below Fourteenth Street—everything's backed up," Charley reported with a shrug.

He went back to listening and I went back to watching the view outside my window.

As the limo glided past Fifty-seventh Street and Henri Bendel, I naturally thought about Lolly Winter. That store is her home away from home.

Thinking about Lolly reminded me that I had promised to escort her to the Fine Arts Ball tonight—and give a speech. Lolly's one of those tireless and civic-minded women who keep New York's nonprofit institutions—not to mention fine department stores—thriving.

"Uh-oh," Charley said suddenly.

"What is it?" I sat up and shifted in the seat to look at him, and he turned the volume up on the radio.

We listened as the reporter announced the latest would-be scandal involving yours truly. It seemed someone had just discovered that the rather obscure wedding chapel at City Hall was going to be the marriage site for the daughter of a very old and loyal friend of mine.

True, in a weak moment I *had* agreed to allow Bevvy Benson to rent the wedding chapel at City Hall for her only daughter's wedding. In an even weaker moment, I had agreed to perform the ceremony. But the city was making money on the deal.

Besides, I admired Bevvy a lot. Smart, savvy, and shrewd, she had managed to carve out a unique career for herself, one of those only-in-New York kinds of things, where as Paperwork, Inc., she acted as an expediter who navigated the intricacies of the city's myriad bureaucracies. She had never used our friendship to do this and she knew that if she did, that would be the end of our relationship.

The radio reporter moved on to a story about premature twins being born on the observation deck of the Empire State Building last night, with the quick-thinking elevator operator who had performed the emergency delivery being hailed as a hero.

"What do you think about this chapel thing?" Charley asked me, lowering the volume.

I threw up my hands. "Ridiculous," I told him. "I've already got a press conference tomorrow—I'll deal with this then."

I leaned back again, thinking that this whole wedding scenario might be one of those headaches that wasn't going to go away.

Rosemary Larkin, with her short salt-and-pepper hair and no-nonsense demeanor, is my number one secretary. She lives in NoHo, the neighborhood just north of Houston Street, and is always pestering me to come down some night so she can take me to a new restaurant that opened last fall on her block. According to Rosemary, they have the best brisket in the city, which of course translates into the best brisket *anywhere*.

Anyone who knows me knows how much I love a good brisket, but I've been too busy lately to take Rosemary up on the offer.

"Morning, Mayor," she said as I walked toward her desk.

"Same to you. What do you have for me?"

"The usual," she said, following me into my office and handing me the day list she'd prepared. "Your first meeting is with that delegation of commuters who want more attention paid to removing the homeless from Grand Central and Penn Station. They're already waiting for you . . ."

I sighed and hung my coat in the big corner closet, then settled into my low-slung black leather armchair. As much as I love my desk, which once belonged to my idol, Mayor La Guardia, I tend to spend a lot of time in this chair, which is the most comfortable piece of furniture I have ever met.

"And Moshe Gur's here, too," Rosemary was saying. "He said—"

"He's early," I interrupted, shaking my head.

"That's what he said. Moshe's always early. But he'll wait."

"He'll have to."

I knew that Moshe, the commissioner of the Department of Housing Preservation and Development, was here with a progress report on the planned sale of the Municipal Railroad Yard to be developed with mixed housing and a riverside park.

With Rosemary standing by, I ran through the rest of the list. A typical day in the life, I thought, scanning past the appointments.

There was one with a delegation of SoHo artists who wanted to legalize all buildings in SoHo and NoHo for artists' studios and residences . . .

And one with Manuel Jimenez, the Parks commissioner, to discuss his ideas for the upcoming annual Easter Egg Roll in Central Park . . .

And . . . ah, there was something to look forward to—lunch!

I was meeting Lou Gregario, commissioner of Sanitation, and Bruno Tonti, head of the Sanitation Workers' Union, to discuss Lou's demand that the sanitation men work a full eight hours and not quit when the truck is full or the route completed.

This meeting I would enjoy, not only because Lou is sharp-witted and sharp-tongued, but because we'd eat—our mutual choice—at the South Street Seaport. I couldn't wait to stuff myself with Peconic Bay scallops, lightly floured, and sauteed in butter and dry sherry.

The thought of it made my stomach rumble.

"Want a bagel?" Rosemary asked promptly. Her ears are just as sharp as those gray eyes of hers behind the silver-framed glasses.

"Sure, I *want* a bagel," I told her, "with chive cream cheese, lox, red onion, the works. But I can't have one." I shook my head and patted my stomach. "I ate a huge meal late last night. Gotta watch it. I already had my morning grapefruit at home."

"How about some coffee, then?"

"That, I'll take."

I finished going over my schedule while Rosemary disappeared into the kitchenette that's off to the side of my office. She returned a few minutes later with a steaming mug and handed it over.

I took a sip and nodded my approval. I make the best coffee in New York, and Rosemary makes the second-best—only because I taught her my secret recipe and specified how important it is to stick to my brand, Martinson's.

"Ready to meet the commuters?" Rosemary asked.

I lifted a shoulder. "Why not?"

With all the headaches—I do get quite a few, though my motto is: I don't *get* headaches; I *give* headaches—I love being mayor and I love being able to do whatever I can to make the city a better place for all the people. For the past three terms plus I've been governing the ungovernable city of New York and, with a little luck, not to mention some appreciation of all the good I've done for the city, I'll be mayor for many more years.

After my last meeting late Thursday afternoon, I finally had a chance to sit down and get some paperwork done. Given the amount of papers to be read and signed, I sometimes think the sole function of government is to produce papers that will never be read again.

Rosemary, her energy and efficiency not the least bit diminished by the long day, came in to read me my messages.

As she worked her way through the sheaf of pink memos, I jotted names and notes on a yellow legal pad.

Finally, she said, "The last one is from Mrs. Laura Gifford Winter."

Lolly. Now *there* was a bright spot.

The woman was one of my dearest friends. We had met through mutual acquaintances a year after her husband died, and I was charmed by her intelligence and wit, not to mention her beauty. It wasn't until a year later that I learned she owned and ran a business that could pay off the city's deficit out of petty cash.

"Mrs. Winter wanted to remind you," Rosemary said, "to pick her up at exactly seven."

The charity fund-raiser tonight. I'd almost forgotten. Lolly was on the Board of Directors of the FAMONY, along with Bevvy Benson.

"Oh, great," I muttered, shaking my head and glancing at my watch. It was already past six. "I'll finish this pile of papers in a few minutes. Would you call Mrs. Winter and tell her I'll be a little late?"

"Of course." Rosemary nodded and walked briskly out of the office.

Tired from the day's irritations and frustrations, I finally initialed the last paper in my IN box, laid it on top of the pile on my left, put the cap on my pen, and began to get up.

Rosemary materialized behind me and pushed me firmly back into my seat. With practiced ease, she placed another pile of papers in front of me. "Scan and initial," she said.

"But I have to pick up Mrs. Winter at seven," I complained. "I'm not even dressed yet. It'll be eight before I pick her up and she has a speech to make and I have a speech to make. And Beverly Benson is running the affair, and she doesn't take anything from anybody."

"Mrs. Winter will wait," Rosemary said, "and so will Mrs. Benson. I know a dozen things I can do to make your life really miserable without even breathing heavy if you're stupid enough not to look at these papers."

I looked her square in the eye. "Nobody threatens me, Rosie; not even you. You could always be fired."

Rosemary smiled smugly. "Good idea, Mayor; then I could earn ten years' pay in an hour from one of the scandal sheets for telling them all about my years with you, not to mention book and movie rights."

"Ridiculous!" I snorted. "You know I've never done any-thing—"

"Depends on how it's written, doesn't it? Now stop wasting time and read."

I gave her the evil eye and reached for the top folder. My hand stopped in midair.

"What's that thick one?" I asked suspiciously.

"The Muni Railroad Yard Project. Mistake. Carol was supposed to put it on the bottom for you to take along." Rosemary pulled the thick folder from mid-pile and put it aside. "Take it with you to read tonight."

"I just told you I'm going out with Mrs. Winter. The fundraising ball, remember? At the Fine Arts Museum? I'm the chief speaker."

"You're right as usual, Boss. You're bound to lose the file if you take it with you, and if the opposition finds it . . . I'll have it messengered to Gracie Mansion; you can read it when you get back from the museum."

"Tonight? Do you know how late it'll be? I suggest you take a nice vacation—not fired; a vacation—for, say, a couple of years. Carol and Jana can easily take over your work. They can even hire an unemployed demon to torture me every hour on the hour to remind me of you."

"I know you're a very quick study," Rosemary said, "but if you think you can memorize everything in this file in less than one night, you're going to have a lot of fun tomorrow morning at the press conference. Of course, if you'd rather look like a complete idiot in front of a big bunch of reporters who'll ask nasty questions about why you're subsidizing Karl Krieg in taking over the biggest real estate deal in the city since the Dutch bought Manhattan, help yourself."

"We're not subsidizing anyone," I said, "particularly not an S.O.B. like Karl Krieg. Sure, the Muni Yard should be developed, but Moshe Gur's going to sell the rights to the highest bidder, with my approval. And you know I'd never let a thief like Krieg get his hands on it."

"One of the things I'm good at, Mayor," Rosemary said, "and you ain't, is picking up scuttlebutt in the ladies' room. There's a rumor that Karl Krieg has retained Paperwork, Inc., to get the project awarded to him without bidding."

"Paperwork, Inc.? Ohmygod, Beverly Benson?"

"Who never loses, teamed up with Karl Krieg, who also never loses."

"How long have you known this?" I asked, suspicious.

"Yesterday morning."

"And you didn't tell me till now?"

"Too busy putting everything in order. Only Carol, Jana, and I know; couldn't trust this to the regular staff. We worked half the night, so make sure you say thank you to Carol and Jana on the way out."

"You checked with Moshe and the corporation counsel and the HPD and the Building Department and—?"

"You trying to teach me my business now?"

"And you want me to read tonight what took the three of you fifteen hours just to put together?"

"Read and *memorize*. You can do it; I've seen you do harder things in less time."

Though I continued to grumble, I had to admit she was absolutely right.

_____ TWO

The following day we gathered for the press conference. The security police detail stood at attention as I led Rosemary Larkin and Moshe Gur, the short, bearded commissioner of Housing Preservation and Development, toward City Hall's main entrance.

I saw the flock of reporters and TV camera crews waiting outside, and knew they were there to grill me. They wanted to catch me unprepared, to show that I didn't know what was going on in my own administration.

As I'd expected, this morning's tabloids had been full of speculation about my link to Bevvy Benson and _her_ link to Karl Krieg and the Muni Yard Project.

The only thing that had kept it off the front pages was a late-breaking scandal about the supposed affair between a local talk show hostess and a very-married celebrity action hero, who was filming his latest movie in Brooklyn.

I was already regretting my favor to Bevvy. Why the heck had I let Lolly Winter talk me into giving Bevvy permission to have her daughter's wedding in the City Hall Chapel? At this point, I really didn't feel like officiating at the civil ceremony just days away. But I knew that everything had been arranged and it would kill Bevvy and her sweet daughter Aileen if I refused.

Meanwhile, the Muni Yard Project program had to be dealt with.

I grabbed hold of Moshe Gur and reminded myself that his somber expression didn't mean we were doomed. With his perpetually solemn dark eyes and full beard that nearly hid his mouth, he always looked serious, even when he was smiling . . . which wasn't often.

"I studied the reports, Moshe," I said, "but you've lived with this. I'd like you to stand out there with me, to answer questions that I can't."

"Sure, Ed," Moshe said. "The HPD is my responsibility."

"One question: Suppose they ask you about Karl Krieg?"

"I'll tell the truth—that he's a crooked, lying monster that the world would be better off without."

"You can't say that, Moshe; the city doesn't need another lawsuit. In fact, if you say that, the project could be tied up in court for years, and may never be built."

"What do you want me to do, Ed?"

"I like Karl Krieg even less than you do; in my first year in office, he developed a turnkey project for us that gave me more trouble than everything else we did that year combined. But you know as well as I do that in front of reporters, we don't give our personal opinions about anyone; we give only indisputable facts."

Moshe raised an eyebrow at me, and I knew what he was thinking. On one or two occasions, I had been known to let a personal opinion or two slip out to a reporter.

All right, so it was more than one or two occasions. In fact, I know full well that I'm not exactly famous for my tact, with reporters—or anyone else.

But the bottom line is that I ultimately know when to keep my mouth shut. That's how I got to be mayor.

And in this particular case, discretion had to be the name of the game.

"I hate and despise Karl Krieg," Moshe was saying, "and you know it's against my religion to lie."

"I accept that, Moshe, so you better stay in here. I don't lie either, but there are ways of presenting the truth that avoid giving your enemies the knife to cut your throat with."

I went out the main entrance of City Hall and stood behind the lectern that had been placed there.

It was another dazzling April morning, cooler than yesterday, but warm enough that most of the reporters grouped in front of City Hall weren't wearing coats.

I saw, as I scanned the faces in the crowd, that almost all of them were familiar, and most looked happy to see me. Why wouldn't they be? Generally speaking, I've done well with the press ever since I took office. It never ceases to amaze me that everything I say is considered news.

"Good morning, ladies and gentlemen of the press," I began. "I always welcome the opportunity to explain and clarify, for those few of you who may have somewhat inaccurate information about certain activities of my administration, what the facts are. It's my understanding that you're all here to focus on a single aspect of our work, the Muni Yard Project, which is a bit surprising since my press office didn't call any of you."

I hesitated and cleared my throat for effect, then added meaningfully, "It almost seems that some person, or his representative, who wanted you all here to discuss the project, called all the papers and TV reporters in town and ordered them to come here. Possibly not ordered; he might have hinted that there would be some sensational news about that project."

I paused again and looked around, then barked, "That is *ridiculous!* To those of you who were fooled, my sympathy. But as long as you're here, so you don't go away empty-handed and have to explain to your editors and producers that you wasted half a day, I can give you some news."

I glanced down at my notes. "This four-billion-dollar project is on the Hudson River, so the Department of Housing Preservation and Development has to get approval from the Environmental Protection Agency and the Army Corps of Engineers. It has to check the old underground maps for streams and soft soil, the Con Ed records for buried utilities, the sewer and water departments for existing mains and their adequacy for the increased population. The required park must be approved by the Department of Parks, the preparatory work is proceeding on schedule, and it looks like it will meet the previously announced due date. Thank you for your attention."

I picked up my papers from the lectern and began straightening them out, as though I were going to leave.

I knew better, of course; none of these reporters would let me go without a struggle or without something quotable.

A very pretty, very young female reporter on the right side of the pack shouted, "There's a rumor that Karl Krieg, with the help of your close friend, Beverly Benson, has made a deal with the city to be given the Muni Railroad Yard for practically nothing. What's your explanation for that, Mr. Mayor?"

"You asked for my explanation of a rumor?" I smiled cordially. "Here it is. Guesswork, of course, but it makes sense. A person with an ax to grind, possibly acting for someone who hopes to get the land himself at a very low price, planted that rumor with a reporter who wasn't experienced enough, or sensible enough, to pick up the phone and call Moshe Gur's office to check the accuracy of the planted story." I turned to the reporters on my left.

"Wait," shouted the young reporter. "You haven't answered my question."

"I certainly have," I said, snapping my head right. "Check your tape recorder. Now please be courteous enough to let the other reporters speak." I turned back toward my left again.

From the group of raised hands, I picked one of the old-timers, a heavyset bearded man wearing glasses.

"Is anyone from your administration," he asked, "preparing to sign a deal with Karl Krieg for the Muni Yard?"

"We aren't preparing to sign a deal with anyone yet," I said, "but we're moving as fast as the legal and regulatory requirements permit to set up an operation by which we hope to get the best deal possible for the city. The Muni Yard is a very valuable piece of property and I want the city to get the maximum benefit from its development."

"Do you intend to sell off the city piece by piece?" another reporter asked.

"That's a ridiculous question and it's also prejudiced, but I'll answer it anyway in the hope that your paper will actually report the answer accurately and completely. Money won't be the only factor in deciding who the developer will be; many other factors will come into play. We'll record the input from all interested parties, but the good of the city will be our goal."

"Will the fact that Mrs. Beverly Benson is your good friend influence your decision?"

"Mrs. Benson *is* my friend. She's also a top-notch professional, and her company, Paperwork, Inc., is one of the best organizations that handles forms and filings with governmental agencies. If she's been retained by Karl Krieg, it's likely that the required horsework and paperwork will be done properly and efficiently. However, there won't be the slightest bit of favoritism shown to Mr. Krieg because I know Mrs. Benson."

I pointed to another reporter.

"Isn't it true," she asked, "that you hate Karl Krieg?"

"Ridiculous! I don't hate any citizen of this city," I said. "I doubt if anyone here has ever heard me use the word 'hate.' And if there were any person in the city that I *disliked,* that person would still be treated fairly in all dealings with the city and its personnel. So if you're trying to find out if Karl Krieg will be given a fair shake when he applies for the right to develop the Muni Yard, you may be sure that he will be treated as well as any other applicant."

There weren't many hands raised, and I was pleased that my tough initial approach had effectively cooled what could have been an embarrassing session.

As I was about to thank the reporters and leave, a man at the back raised his hand.

"Isn't it a fact, Mr. Mayor," he asked, "that Mrs. Benson has been up before a Grand Jury twice on possible charges of bribery? Will this affect the way Karl Krieg's work is processed in the various departments that have jurisdiction?"

"Each time Mrs. Benson has been called before a Grand Jury," I said, "it was in response to accusations from two people who had been fired for incompetence. There was no evidence of wrongdoing and, in the opinion of other witnesses, they seemed to have collaborated on their claims. Some columnists felt that the accusations were instigated by a rival of Mrs. Benson's, but there was no proof of this."

I took a deep breath. "Let me put this to rest once and for all, not just because I'm friendly with Mrs. Benson, and not just because I believe very strongly in justice, but because an accusation of bribery by anyone who does business with the city is also an accusation that a member of this administration has accepted a bribe. I don't care what job a servant of the people holds; to my mind he must be purer than the average citizen. If he or she takes a free doughnut or a free hot dog, that person is gone the moment I find out about it. Because Mrs. Benson is a friend, I had all her transactions with this administration double-checked by two different teams. I was told it was the skill and knowledge of her associates that allowed her papers and permits to be processed efficiently at maximum speed."

The same reporter asked, "Didn't you give Mrs. Benson permission to hold her daughter's wedding in the City Hall Chapel this Sunday?"

"Yes, I did," I snapped, "and she paid a fee like anyone else."

"Will there be any city officials at the wedding," someone else asked, "and will that count as a gratuity given by someone doing business with the city?"

Another provocative question, but nothing I'm not experienced enough to handle.

"I will instruct whatever city officials have been invited to have a miserable time, to make sure a waiter spills soup on their heads, and to get food poisoning," I assured them. "I will also ask Mrs. Benson to invite you and to make sure you get that same treatment so that you won't feel obligated to write favorably about the wedding or the bride's gown."

I signaled "enough" with both hands and said, "Good day. Thank you for coming." Then I turned around and went back into City Hall.

Moshe Gur got to me first. "If any of those fools," he said, "thinks I can be pressured into—"

"Don't worry," I said. "Do what's right and keep me up-to-date."

Shaking his head, Gur walked away.

Rosemary Larkin added her two cents. "You know, you really don't have to insult reporters; they have nothing to do but make trouble for you."

"You want me to encourage them? I think it helps to show up the incompetent fools and the prejudiced ones."

Rosemary shook her head and went back to her office.

But I could see the matter was not going to fade away.

THREE

The night of the wedding, the police security guards at the main entrance of City Hall waved me and my Gang of Five around the metal detector line, and Lolly too; it was clear that she couldn't possibly be carrying a weapon in her little clutch bag.

"I love weddings," Lolly confided to me as we all walked downstairs. She was dolled up in one of her trademark clingy, off-the-shoulder evening gowns. Her short blond hair was curled and arranged to frame her artfully made-up face, and she oozed expensive perfume. "Don't you love weddings, Ed?"

"Why not?" I said with a shrug, thinking that I loved them a lot more when I didn't have to officiate and when they didn't give me as much political grief as this one already had.

"Bevvy says Aileen and Alan are thrilled that you're performing the civil ceremony," Lolly said, as though she had read my mind. "They'll always remember it. This was really sweet of you, Ed."

"Yeah, well, I'm a sweet guy."

"I'll bet Aileen will be a beautiful bride. Bevvy had the gown custom made for her by Verna Chung."

"By *who?*"

"Verna Chung?" Lolly said, as though she was trying to prod my memory. When I shrugged, she sighed and shook her head.

"She's only the most famous wedding dress designer in the city, Ed."

Now I ask you, how would I know that? Sometimes Lolly baffles me.

At the bottom of the stairs we found another uniformed police guard just outside the door to the chapel. Two bathrooms were directly across the corridor behind the guard and, at the far end of the corridor, about fifty feet away, was the basement exit, protected by another metal detector and another guard.

There was a large white van parked just outside this door, and the men and women of the caterer's crew, in white tuxedos and white gloves, were bringing in covered containers, trays, plastic plates and glasses, utensils, and a big container of paper napkins.

The bartenders, identified by the white aprons around their waists, were rolling in barrels of ice and beer on dollies, and pushing along a grand piano–sized bar on casters that had, on its enclosed shelves, the bottles of wine and hard liquor, the mixers, the nuts and nibbles, the cherries, the presliced lemons and limes, the olives, and the pearl onions.

Charley Deacon and one of my other bodyguards went into the chapel to introduce themselves to the caterer and to check for assassins and bombs, two more checked the bathrooms, and one went out the back to look over the delivery operation.

"We're early," I observed.

"Bevvy wanted me—us—here early," Lolly said. "So let's go in." As she pushed open the door with a manicured hand, the light caught the precious stones on her enormous cocktail ring and the ruby bracelet her husband had given her for their anniversary.

Remembering that Lolly had been married once, I felt a soft spot for her. After all, here she was, a widow at a wedding.

"Oh, Ed, look!" she breathed, stopping in the doorway as we entered the chapel.

It was barely recognizable. The small alcoves on all four sides of the chapel, which had been covered by heavy, dingy, ragged curtains, were now gleaming with broad shiny white linen, artfully hung and draped across each opening to hide the old curtains and to harmonize with the wedding theme.

The ceiling had been freshly painted in matte white and, to help brighten the windowless room, there were high, standing photographer's lights, with reflectors, spotted along the walls between the alcoves. Big baskets of exotic out-of-season flowers stood on carved white-painted wooden pedestals in the corners of the room and between the alcoves in front of the tall lights.

Near the only entrance to the chapel, Lolly and I saw that a young woman, also in a white tuxedo but identified as the boss-lady by the red carnation in her buttonhole, was speaking to Beverly.

"I'm sorry, Mrs. Benson," she was saying, "but there are no facilities here to let us provide anything hot and there is no way to use silverware or china or glass for the cold food and drink."

"But you said you'd try to—"

"If we can't heat anything to a safe temperature, and if we can't wash anything or sterilize anything, we have to use disposable plastic. We won't even serve anything that's been out of the van refrigerator more than an hour. How would you like it if the mayor got salmonella poisoning?"

I shuddered at the thought.

Meanwhile, Bevvy pressed on, "But I wanted damask napkins and—"

"I guarantee that your guests will be happy," Miss Red Carnation said confidently. "The hors d'oeuvres are delicious and original, the drinks are of the highest quality and will be mixed perfectly to the taste of each guest, the champagne for the wedding toast will be Dom Perignon, the service will be unobtrusive but watchful, and there will be more than enough of everything for everybody."

"I'm sure there will, but—"

"I don't mean to be critical, Mrs. Benson, but you picked Fab Affairs because we're the finest and we'll prove it to you in every way. Twenty minutes after the last guest leaves, you won't know we've been here; the chairs will be neatly stacked back in the alcoves, there won't be a crumb on the floor or a napkin behind the flowers. We'll vacuum the corridor and we'll even clean the bathrooms across the hall."

"But . . . But . . ." For once, Bevvy's voice failed her.

"You're just having first-wedding jitters, Mrs. Benson. It's perfectly normal. But you're paying us top dollar to do a perfect job and we will do a perfect job. So go and enjoy this occasion." The young woman pointed to us. "Your first guests have arrived and they're waiting for you to greet them. There will be more coming every second."

"Oh, Lolly, Ed." Bevvy turned and saw us hovering in the doorway. She and Lolly kissed the air near each other's cheeks.

"Witch," Bevvy said. "Do you always have to look better than I do?"

Bevvy, of course, looked every bit the glamorous mother of the bride. She wore a shimmering salmon-colored gown that hugged her figure, and her dark hair was pulled back into a smooth chignon. Under her arm was a sparkly, beaded, champagne-colored clutch purse.

She air-kissed me next. "Ed, you don't know how excited Aileen is that you're doing the wedding ceremony. She could barely sleep last night."

"Thanks for the flattery, Bevvy, but maybe that had more to do with the groom and the fact that she's about to get married than it does with me," I said dryly.

Bevvy chuckled and took Lolly's arm. "Can I talk to you for a second?"

"Uh-oh," Lolly said. "What is it? Whenever you say that . . ."

"Don't look at me like that. I'm serious, Lolly. You have to do something for the good of the wedding," Bevvy said earnestly.

"For Aileen I'd do anything. But I've learned, since I made the mistake of rooming with you at Bennington when I was young and foolish, that when you say it's for the good of someone, it's for the bad of me."

"Not really. At least, not this time. Listen, Alan's mother, May Lang, told me that her husband, Ken, is a little nervous today. You know Ken, don't you?" she asked both of us.

Lolly nodded.

I thought about it, and said, "I think I met him once, at that New Year's Eve party Lolly had. Tall, thin, balding, glasses?"

"That's Ken. Anyway, May was afraid to make him take tranquilizers because everybody'll be drinking all day long and he'll probably put away a few gallons himself without even thinking.

After all, he's the father of the groom. He and Alan are very close. In fact, last summer they—"

"Just where do I fit in here?" Lolly cut in.

"What I want you to do is sort of hang around him—not such a terrible job; he's really very sweet—most of the time, but not so he'd notice it. Keep him amused and entertained, and see that he doesn't drink too much."

"That's all?" Lolly asked suspiciously.

"That's all. Just be charming and beautiful—you really do look super-gorgeous today—and listen to him like you're interested. You've done it before with lots of boring men. We all have."

"Didn't you once tell me Ken Lang is an accountant?" Lolly asked.

"A tax consultant with a wide range of cultural interests."

"Why can't his wife . . . ?"

"She's the mother of the groom. She has to—"

Lolly cut her short again. "Bull. She has ten seconds in the spotlight, then she fades into the wallpaper. It's the mother of the bride who has the lead part, and you know it, Bevvy." She shot Bevvy a level look. "The real reason, or I walk."

Lolly, I thought admiringly, is nothing if not sharp.

Bevvy hesitated. "Okay. You look so sexy that—"

"The *primary* real reason, liar."

"Ed, would you excuse us?"

What could I say? "Sure, go ahead. I'll just stand here alone and admire the decor."

"It is lovely, isn't it?" Bevvy missed my sarcasm, as usual.

She took a deep breath and pulled Lolly out of my earshot.

I kept an eye on them, because after all, how interesting, after the first glance, is a room filled with flowers and white linen draperies?

Bevvy was clearly trying to talk Lolly into something and Lolly was clearly not going to do it. Then, apparently, Bevvy told Lolly something that made her give in.

At that moment, a couple entered the chapel, and I recognized the parents of the groom.

"Oh, May, Ken, you're here!" Beverly called, and hurried over to them, sweeping Lolly along with her.

I joined them, and Bevvy made reintroductions all around.

"Mr. Mayor, you don't know how pleased we are that you're going to perform our son's marriage ceremony," May said graciously. "Alan is so honored."

"I'm glad."

"And so is Aileen," Bevvy reminded me again. "May, you have to come and see the flowers. They're exquisite. Rafael did exactly what we had in mind with the roses and ivy."

"Good. Just let me put my purse down," May said, and waved the navy drawstring bag that exactly matched the fabric of her sleek gown. She headed toward the front of the chapel.

Lolly, I noticed, was already somehow deep in conversation with Ken Lang, about who knew what. One thing about Mrs. Laura Winter—she can charm just about anyone, including nervous accountants.

She guided Ken into the far corner to my right at the back of the chapel, and stood in front of him, talking.

Bevvy turned to me and whispered, "Part of the deal is that you have to go over to Lolly every five minutes and be charming."

"I'm automatically charming," I said. "I can't help it. But what's the plot you've obviously hatched?"

"Just girl stuff," Bevvy said. "It's on a need-to-know basis. And you don't need to know." She hurried off to meet May.

I knew her; there was no way for me to get any useful information from her until she was good and ready.

Since the bar wasn't yet open, I decided to go for a walk, and headed out of the chapel and back up to the main entrance.

There, I chatted with the security officers for a few minutes. I see most of them every day, and it's not often that I have a chance to stop and talk. I'm usually rushing by them, in a hurry to get to a meeting, or escape the reporters who so often camp out on the steps in front.

"Here come some wedding guests," Tony, one of the officers, announced after a little while, pointing at the Town Car that had just dispatched a couple clad in a tux and gown.

They walked up to the entrance and the man said, "Ed, how are you?"

"Great," I said, not recognizing him. "How'm I doin'?"

"You know I've always wanted to meet him so that I could hear him say that in person," the guy said to his wife as he deposited his keys and change in the plastic tub, then walked through the metal detector.

"We're the Lewises, Margot and Tim—friends of the Bensons," the woman said.

"Nice to meet you."

"Ma'am," Tony said, offering her a basket, "would you please place your bag in here?"

"Of course." She put her satin clutch in.

"I have to open it," Tony told her as she stepped through the detector.

"Feel free," Margot Lewis invited, and he snapped open the clasp, quickly inspected the inside, and handed it back.

"Tony, I'll see you later," I told him, and accompanied the Lewises back down to the chapel.

When we got there, Bevvy was waiting to greet them.

In the corner, Lolly and Ken Lang were still chattering away. Rather, Lolly was chattering, and Ken was listening.

I noticed that the waiters were starting to make their rounds with cold snacks and the bar had opened for action, so I strolled over.

May was there, ordering a tall, weak gin and tonic, when I arrived at her elbow.

"I notice that your husband," I said, "seems very interested in Lolly Winter."

"I'm glad," May said. "She's very sweet."

Another group of guests came in right then.

"Would you excuse me, Ed? Those are my in-laws, and I really should go over to say hello."

"Of course."

She left to stand near the chapel entrance.

I ordered a brandy, then headed over to where May and Bevvy were greeting the guests. They had been joined by Bevvy's husband, Ralph, a short, round, pleasant-faced man whose booming laugh kept rising above the polite chitchat.

I hung back a little, but stayed close enough to overhear anything interesting, which is an old habit of mine. It especially comes in handy during elections.

"Caviar, Mr. Mayor?" asked a passing waiter, offering me a tray.

"Thank you."

I kept an eye on Ken and Lolly and an ear to the conversation by the door, and balanced my drink in one hand as I popped the cracker into my mouth.

Delicious.

I realized, as I munched, that I was famished, as usual.

"Smoked salmon?" someone else asked, and I helped myself, then turned around just in time to see Moshe Gur and his wife come in.

I watched and listened as Beverly introduced her husband, Ralph, to them.

Ruth Gur, a very attractive woman in her mid-thirties, was wearing a simple gray evening gown. Beneath her arm was a flat, rectangular, gray brocade purse, and her dark hair was caught back in a bow made of similar fabric.

"Everything here and at the Plaza will be kosher," Bevvy was telling Ruth, "so enjoy."

"That's very thoughtful of you," Ruth said with a smile. "Thanks."

"It's not just for you," Ralph Benson said. "We want to make sure that all our guests have a good time and don't have to worry about what they're eating."

Moshe Gur looked around the room nervously. He found me and came over to say hello. "Good afternoon, Ed."

I smiled. "Your wife looks wonderful. I'm glad she could come."

"Ruth always looks wonderful," Moshe said proudly, then lowered his voice. "I know this is a social occasion, but can I have a few words with you as the mayor?"

"Even here?" I sighed. "I was hoping that . . . Okay, but there are very few people I'd do it for. What is it?"

"Same as before. How to stop Krieg. You said you had a solution, an idea, but you'd have to work out the details. Have you done that yet?"

"Most of the details, yes, but I need the cooperation of your department and—"

"That's no problem."

"Let me finish, Moshe; I also need the cooperation of the City Council, particularly that of the speaker of the Council."

Gur looked stunned. "But they'll never cooperate."

I smiled and plucked a chopped liver appetizer off a passing waiter's tray. "They will. A little horse trading, a little pressure, a little promise of support in the next election . . . They'll work with me. Don't worry."

"Thank you, Mr. Mayor," Gur said through tight lips, and walked back to his wife.

Ruth was talking to a short gray-haired woman, Joan Mardin, and her tall gray-haired husband, Frank.

Joan and her husband, I knew, were developers for the Jomar Development Corporation, a pretty good firm. They had done a subsidized housing job for the city in my third term and, though I'd never met them, I was satisfied with their work.

Still, knowing how stiff-necked her husband was, Ruth Gur shouldn't have been talking to Joan Mardin at all, innocent though it probably was.

When Moshe went over to get his wife, I could see Ruth introduce her husband to both Mardins. Moshe was too polite to interrupt the introductions, but as soon as they were over he clearly made some kind of excuse, took Ruth's arm, and led her away.

From the color of the back of his neck it was obvious he was telling his wife that she must never even say "Hello" to any builder or developer.

I really think that's carrying things too far, but I'd rather have a commissioner who bends over backward to avoid even the appearance of favoritism than one who thinks the letter of the law is for lesser mortals.

I was about to head over toward Lolly and Ken Lang when someone tapped my shoulder.

"Ed," a familiar voice said behind me, and I turned to see Gil Cardone, an old friend of mine.

"Gil, good to see you," I said, and spent the next fifteen minutes or so chatting with him about his new granddaughter and the house he and his wife were building up in Dutchess County.

"I know what you think of the country, Ed," he said, "but Dolores and I—"

"You don't have to make apologies to me, Gil. It's beyond me why you'd want to spend a bundle on a piece of property in the middle of nowhere, but that's your business. Just don't invite me to visit."

He grinned. "I was just about to, but I guess I'll hold off."

His eyes bulged slightly then, and I turned and followed his gaze toward the entrance just in time to see Karl Krieg come in. I'd recognize his squatty body and fat face anywhere. With him was a tall, spectacularly beautiful woman in a red dress.

"Who is *that?*" Gil asked, staring.

"Donna Krieg, Karl's wife. She used to be a showgirl in Vegas."

"Yeah, I've read about her."

"Who hasn't?"

The billionaire developer's voluptuous young wife tended to be almost as much a fixture in the tabloids as I was.

"Mr. Mayor?" a voice said behind me, and I turned to see a tuxedo-clad man standing there, wielding a camera. The wedding photographer, obviously.

"I'm Don O'Sullivan," he said, "and this is Kerry Worthy, my assistant." He indicated the petite, short-haired blonde who was with him, holding a light meter. "Can we get a shot of you for the official wedding album?"

"Of course." I obliged by slinging an arm around Gil's shoulder and posing for the camera with a big, undoubtedly cheesy smile.

"Thank you, sir. And by the way, even though you didn't ask me, you're doing a great job," Don O'Sullivan informed me before darting off to capture a shot of the bride's grandmother, who had just come in.

"Listen, I'm going up to the bar," Gil announced. "Can I get you anything?"

"No, thanks," I said, swirling what was still left in my glass and taking a sip.

As soon as he'd left, I slid a little closer to the door so that I was in earshot of what was happening there.

Donna Krieg was being greeted warmly by Bevvy. I could see how gracefully Bevvy avoided shaking hands with Krieg—an interesting development, given the questions I had been asked at the press conference two days ago—even as she complimented Donna on her eye-catching gown.

Donna Krieg, from what I could see of Bevvy's treatment of her, was a truly poised and polite young woman. What she was doing married to a coarse crook like Karl Krieg was beyond me.

Bevvy turned to greet another guest, and I saw Krieg casing the room.

His eyes clearly fell on Moshe Gur. Shamelessly he pointed his wife toward the HPD commissioner.

Was this why Donna was wearing that dress? For Moshe Gur? And with Ruth in the room?

Krieg was not only a crook, but stupid to boot.

"Ed, is that you?" someone asked, and I reluctantly forced my attention away from the Kriegs.

"Oh, Helene, how are you?" I greeted Bevvy's Park Avenue neighbor.

As I chatted with her, and then with another couple whom I'd met at the fund-raising ball Thursday night, I managed to keep tabs on the Kriegs.

I saw Donna go to the bar and order a drink.

Meanwhile, Karl cased the area and zeroed in on the Mardins. Shouldering his way through the now-crowded room, Krieg walked right up to Frank and Joan. Frank made a disgusted face and pulled away to go to the bar. I noticed he had a slight limp.

Joan Mardin didn't look very happy, as Krieg was clearly trying to sweet-talk her. They had been speaking for a few minutes when Joan looked aside and waved to her husband. Frank, looking angry, started to walk toward her. Krieg turned, saw Frank approaching, and quickly walked away.

"It must be almost time for the ceremony to start," the woman I had been chatting with said, and nudged her husband. "Darryl, why don't we go over and say a quick hello to May? It's going to be too difficult to pin her down later."

"Good idea. We'll see you at the reception at the Plaza, Ed," her husband said, shaking my hand.

"See you there." I nodded as they walked off, and looked around the room.

Lolly and Ken Lang, I noticed, had been joined by several guests.

Lolly caught my eye and arched a perfectly plucked brow as if to say, "where have you been?"

I took a step in her direction and was promptly waylaid by someone who claimed to have been good friends with my father, Bernie, back when he was the number one waiter at the Merkin Deli on West Fifty-eighth Street.

I nodded and said all the right things, still scanning the room out of the corner of my eye.

Over by the door, I saw that Beverly Benson was holding a list and checking off guests' arrivals. She handed the list to her husband and signaled Miss Red Carnation.

I looked around for Charley Deacon, and saw that he was also standing near the entrance. Two of the detectives were outside in the corridor, and two more were standing against the wall on the corridor side of the chapel.

Two minutes after Bevvy signaled the caterer, all the food and drink disappeared, and the waiters went around collecting the plastic glasses, swizzle sticks, plates, toothpicks, and napkins in plastic sacks.

This done, Miss Red Carnation loudly announced that the chairs would now be brought out and asked the guests not to sit down until all the chairs were in place so that the seating could be set up quickly and properly.

"Well, I guess I'll go find the wife," my father's old pal said, clapping me on the back. "See you after the ceremony."

I gave a jovial wave.

A moment later, I found myself caught in the throng of guests, who squeezed themselves against the walls of the chapel as the caterer's people began taking the folding chairs from the draped alcoves. They set them up in two rectangles with a wide aisle between them leading from the corridor entrance to the front of the chapel.

When the chairs were lined up properly, a lectern was set up at the front of the chapel and the guests were allowed to sit down. There was some confusion as people jockeyed to get the front row seats, but it lasted only a couple of minutes.

I kept watching Lolly. As soon as the first chairs were being brought out, she sneaked away from Ken Lang and stood at the front of the room. The moment the game of musical chairs started, she was already in her front row seat, on the bride's side of the lectern.

I was waiting with my back to the corridor wall, keeping my practiced eye on the audience. When all the guests were fully settled in their seats, I walked slowly, with appropriate dignity, down the aisle to the lectern. There, I delivered some introductory remarks about the families that were about to be joined.

I then asked Mr. and Mrs. Lang and Mr. and Mrs. Benson to retire to the corridor just outside the chapel, leaving the pair of doors open. From that position, they would escort the bride and groom to the municipal altar, where I would unite them.

When everyone was in place, I nodded toward the corridor.

The pale and clearly nervous young groom and his best man came down the aisle and stood before the lectern.

A minute later, the flushed and adorable bride, accompanied by her father and mother, came halfway down the aisle. She looked lovely in her elaborate white gown, if I do say so myself.

Alan came to take her from her parents and escort her to the ritual area before the lectern.

I went through a very short ceremony, closing it with, ". . . and by the powers vested in me by the State of New York, I pronounce you man and wife. You may kiss the bride."

As the bride and groom were kissing enthusiastically, the guests applauded wildly and a few, inspired by the ceremony, formal and legalistic though it was, also kissed enthusiastically.

The bride and groom walked back down the aisle and the guests started to get up.

"One moment, please." I raised my hands and said, "Will everyone please remain seated a little longer?" The servers began pouring and passing out plastic flutes of champagne. "I want to offer a toast to the bride and groom. Will everyone please rise? Thank you."

I waited a moment, then raised my glass. The crowd followed suit, and I saw Don O'Sullivan snapping away from the back of the chapel.

"I wish for the bride and groom, Aileen and Alan," I said, blinking from the flashbulbs, "everything they wish for themselves. And for the parents of the happy couple, Kenneth and May Lang, and Ralph and Beverly Benson, a wish that they will see in their children a continuation of the happiness they've found in their own unions."

Old-fashioned, maybe, but I believe a solemn occasion should not be demeaned by jokes and supposedly clever sayings.

I took a long drink of champagne, then announced, "Just outside the exit is a fleet of limousines that will take you all to the Plaza, where the *real* celebration will begin. See you there."

As the guests began to leave, I went over to Lolly, who was still sitting on the bride's side of the aisle.

"For a formal bureaucratic ceremony," she said, "it was delivered lovingly, Ed. Did you have a nice time at the cocktail hour?"

"I always do. I tried to work my way over to you so that I could be charming to Ken Lang, but I kept getting waylaid."

Lolly shrugged. "That's what happens when you're mayor. Don't worry about it; I survived."

"You always do," I told her, and looked around.

Moshe, who was just about to walk out the door with Ruth, gave me a wave and a nod that meant, "we'll talk at the reception."

Nearby, I spotted Donna Krieg and heard her ask Bevvy if she knew where Karl had gone.

"No, I don't," Bevvy said, "but I'm sure he's around this mad rush someplace. Why don't you grab a seat in a limo, and I'll tell him that you've gone ahead when he turns up?"

Donna, I noticed, didn't look all that upset at the prospect of leaving her husband behind.

Poor kid, I thought, watching as she sashayed her red dress out the door. What was she doing married to that creep? I wondered again. Everyone knew Krieg had a string of bimbos from here to the Hamptons.

I spent the next ten minutes shaking hands as people passed me on the way out, telling me how wonderful the ceremony had been done.

"My Bunny is getting married next winter," a friend of Lolly's told me glowingly. "You remember her, don't you, Ed? She had an internship at City Hall a few years back. Anyway, we'd *love* to have you officiate at her wedding."

I smiled and mumbled something polite and noncommittal, wondering, not for the first time, why I'd ever agreed to do Bevvy this favor.

"Ed," Lolly said, touching my sleeve, when the room had almost cleared out, "are you ready to go?"

I nodded.

Miss Red Carnation, seeing that just about everyone had left, signaled her crew to start cleaning up and putting away the chairs. Lolly and I left the chapel, and accompanied by my five bodyguards, walked slowly down the hall toward the limos.

Suddenly, one of the caterer's young men ran out and grabbed Charley Deacon, pulled him back and whispered into his ear.

Charley barked, "Surround. Weapons," and ran back to the chapel.

The other four detectives pushed me and Lolly against the wall, turned their backs on us to make a living protective wall, and drew their handguns.

"What's happening?" Lolly asked, looking wide-eyed at the weapons.

"Nothing, probably," I said to reassure her. "But we have to do what Charley says. When he thinks something has to be done, he outranks me."

A few seconds later, Charley opened the chapel door. "Okay, come in here."

We all started moving as a unit, and Lolly clutched my jacket, obviously frightened.

"Just the mayor," he said, holding up a hand like a traffic cop. "You guys stay with Mrs. Winter."

As I walked to the door, Charley was placing a call on his portable phone. It was a short call, and he bent his head and muffled his voice so that I couldn't hear a word he was saying.

Then he quickly put away the phone and held the door open for me. "Okay, Mayor, come on."

In the chapel, the caterer's people, looking upset—one of the tuxedo-clad women was crying—were sitting in the chairs, only half of which had been put away. Even Miss Red Carnation looked flustered.

Deacon led me to one of the alcoves at the back of the chapel. Carefully, with a clean plastic spoon, he pulled back the curtain.

Karl Krieg was sitting on the floor, slumped against the sidewall of the alcove with his head on his chest. A slim, narrow steel blade, the end wrapped in a paper napkin to make a handle, was stuck in Krieg's chest under the ribs near his breastbone.

Around the blade, his dress shirt was covered with bright red blood, and the bloodied napkin was soaking up the slow flow of his life.

____FOUR

Charley Deacon nervously brushed back his gray hair from his sweaty forehead and looked at me.

He had led me back to a tiny room adjacent to the chapel, where I'd immediately sunk into the first chair I saw, still shaken by the sight of Karl Krieg with that knife sticking out of his chest.

"I, uh, need to ask you a few questions, Ed," Charley said. "Other than the catering crew—and I can interrogate them later—you and Mrs. Winter are the only witnesses around."

He was fiddling with a pencil, tapping it against the arm of his chair, obviously jittery.

And no wonder.

I didn't envy his position. After all, he was a police officer in charge of four other men, all of them with nothing to do but watch a very small crowd of very important people in a very small room with no windows and only one exit—a room in which a rich and prominent man had been murdered right under his nose.

He was undoubtedly thinking that he'd be lucky, when this was over, to be put on traffic duty in Harlem.

Not to mention the news articles and the editorials calling for the resignation of the police commissioner, which would also inevitably be blamed on him by all the remaining brass.

And, of course, after that happened, the blame would eventually fall on me, because when you're mayor, it always does.

"Okay, Charley," I said, determined to make this easy on both of us. "Shoot."

He looked grateful. "You understand that I'm not accusing you, Mayor; I know better than anyone else how straight you are."

I nodded; that went without saying.

"But I've got to go by the book, here. I need some information while your memory's fresh." He took out his notebook. "I know your name and address, so let's start with this: who is the deceased?"

I figured he probably knew that—few people in New York wouldn't recognize the guy—but obliged by saying, "Karl Krieg. He's a developer."

"I've heard of him before: all bad. Did you notice anything suspicious here today?"

I contemplated that. "As you probably know, I spent most of my time before the ceremony shaking hands and greeting old friends . . ."

"Did you shake hands with the deceased?"

"It so happened that our paths never crossed," I said truthfully.

"You avoided him?"

"You said it; I didn't. No one will ever see me acting as though I'm deliberately avoiding any citizen."

"Don't I know it," Charley said. "While you weren't *not* deliberately avoiding Mr. Krieg, did you notice him talking to anybody? Having an argument with anybody? Threatening gestures? Bad attitudes?"

"When he came in, I saw him introducing himself and his wife, Donna—she was the one who was almost wearing the red dress—to Beverly and Ralph Benson. As you know, the bride was their daughter—the Benson's daughter—Aileen."

Deacon was still focused on Donna. "The red dress? Yeah, I know the lady you mean. Hard to miss her. I saw her talking to Commissioner Gur."

"Well, knowing Moshe, he wasn't fazed by her."

"Commissioner Gur doesn't go for that stuff?"

"Commissioner Gur doesn't go for any kind of stuff. He's very—very Orthodox."

"He'd get mad if anybody tried to con him into doing something he thought was wrong? Something that was against his religion, maybe?"

"Yes. That is, no, not mad the way you mean."

"How do you know the way I mean, Mayor?" He waited a moment, then said, "Let's get back to what I asked you about Mr. Krieg. Did you see him talking to anybody? Arguing with anybody? Making threatening gestures? Anything like that?"

"Nothing."

Charley nodded, examined his notebook, and apparently decided to try a different track. "Your escort, Mrs. Winter, seemed to be monopolizing Mr. Lang. I happened to notice that, like I notice anything that doesn't fit. Mr. Lang's not particularly handsome or amusing—I didn't see Mrs. Winter laugh even once—so why should she hang around him, especially when you were around?"

"Bevvy asked Mrs. Winter to talk to him. I guess he was nervous. After all, this was his son's wedding. I'm sure Mrs. Benson or Mrs. Winter will be able to tell us more about that— Which reminds me," I said. "Mrs. Winter is still out in the hall. How about bringing her in here so she can sit down? She should know why we're being held up. She must be really worried by now."

"I'll bring her here in a minute. So did you see anything else that was suspicious?"

"Else?" I'm a lawyer, and that kind of loaded question won't get a lot of cooperation from me. "I didn't see *anything* at all suspicious, Charley, I told you. But some things are clear."

"And those things are . . . ?"

"The murder wasn't committed while the chairs were in their alcoves; Mr. Krieg was on the floor in the corner of the alcove. That was where the catering crew reached in for the stacks of chairs. So it could only have been done after all the chairs were set up. Right?"

"Right."

I was on a roll. "It couldn't have been Mrs. Winter because she was in the front seat as soon as the guests were allowed to sit down. On the left side as I was facing the lectern."

"Mrs. Winter was never a suspect, Mayor; I had two men in the hall, but three of us were standing with our backs to the rear wall and I myself saw Mrs. Winter waiting in the front row. First seat on the left side of the aisle, like you said."

"And since you guys were watching me, it couldn't have been me either." Might as well settle that now.

"For the record, I personally wasn't watching you the whole time, but I do know that you were near the back wall, sort of to my right."

"I assure you, Charley, it wasn't me; I was busy keeping an eye on the front of the room to see when I could go up there to perform the wedding ceremony."

"I told you, Mayor, I know how straight you are. I just have to—"

"I know, I know." My mind was racing. "Listen, Charley, think about this. It couldn't have been anyone who was in the chapel. That knife looked like steel to me, and everyone here had to pass through the metal detector to get in. We have the latest, most sensitive models; that's something the City Council always votes for. The thought of some angry taxpayer wanting to express his opposition to some councilman the hard way is a very powerful persuader to approving these expenditures."

"It should be," Charley said with a nod. "So every guest passed through the detector, except the five of us and you and Mrs. Winter. Remember, they just waved us past." He hesitated.

"Charley, you don't think Lolly was an accomplice."

He quickly shook his head. "Unless somebody slipped something into her bag or into your pocket, and then took it back later."

"That's ridiculous! You five were surrounding us from the moment we picked up Mrs. Winter until we went into the chapel."

"I'm just checking out all the possibilities."

"*Im*possibilities. But I know, I know, you're just doing your job. Still, look at it this way: Why would Karl Krieg go into an alcove with anybody?"

"A woman, maybe? From what I heard of him, that's one way he got his kicks."

I considered that. "I doubt it. The best-looking woman here was his own wife, Donna. The rumor is that he wasn't on good terms with her, but that doesn't mean anything. Besides his wife, there *were* some attractive women here. . . . Lolly, for one, and

Bevvy Benson, May Lang, and Ruth Gur, but . . ." I trailed off and shook my head.

"Mrs. Benson has been linked to Mr. Krieg through a recent business deal, though," Charley said, rubbing his chin and looking at me.

"Believe me, Charley, there is no way that Bevvy Benson, who was the mother of the bride to begin with, and who didn't like Krieg, would. . . . No, that's just too crazy."

"But Krieg and Mrs. Benson *were* in a big business deal together."

"That doesn't mean they liked each other. Or didn't."

Deacon checked his notebook. "How about May Lang? Was Mrs. Winter keeping her husband busy so she could sneak off for a quickie?"

"How can the mother of the groom sneak off at her own son's wedding? Besides, she's not the type, especially with a creep like Karl Krieg."

"You know her that well?"

"Today is maybe the fifth time I met her, but I can tell."

"So why did Mrs. Winter have to keep Mr. Lang busy?"

"I already told you, because Mr. Lang was nervous. I'm sure Mrs. Winter will be able to give you more information about that."

Deacon checked his notes again. "How about Ruth Gur in the alcove with Krieg?"

"An Orthodox woman? Who thinks it's a sin just to carry keys or money on the Sabbath? And whose husband hates Karl Krieg?"

"She's Commissioner Gur's wife and he hates the deceased . . ."

"I didn't mean hates," I corrected, "as in *hates*. I meant he considered Krieg's company insufficiently qualified to do city work."

"And you said you were standing near the alcove where Krieg got stabbed when the chairs were being set up?"

"I was concentrating on the front area where I was going to marry the young couple and I was waiting for all the guests to settle down so I could go to the lectern." I thought for a moment, then said, "So you *are* considering me as a suspect?"

"I told you, Mayor, I was just hoping you might have seen something."

"I was focused on the lectern, not looking sideways."

He closed his notebook and stood up. "Thanks for your help."

"But I didn't do anything; I only pointed out a few things that were obvious."

"You were very helpful. The medical examiner will be here soon, and then we'll know a lot more." He went to the door and stuck his head out.

"Will you send in Mrs. Winter, please?" he asked the officer posted outside, then turned back to me. "Mayor, you'll have to wait outside while I talk to her."

"But—"

"You know that witnesses can't be questioned together. And you and Mrs. Winter are both witnesses."

What could I do but agree to step outside as Lolly, looking puzzled, appeared in the doorway.

"What's going on?" she asked, looking from me to Charley.

"Have a seat, Mrs. Winter."

Charley sat her in the chair I had used, and sat down opposite her. Then he gave me a pointed look.

Reluctantly, I left the room, closing the door firmly behind me.

"You can wait in there, Mr. Mayor," the cop outside told me, motioning toward a small alcove nearby.

"Thank you." I walked over and took a seat against the wall . . . the apparently and conveniently paper-*thin* wall that happened to border the room where Charley was questioning Lolly.

I knew this because I heard every word they said, as clearly as if I was in there with them.

"I'm sorry," Charley apologized, "to delay your going to the wedding party with your friends but. . . . There's no easy way to say it: There's been a homicide. Mr. Karl Krieg."

Lolly sounded startled. "Karl Krieg is dead?"

"Yes."

"Oh."

"You're not upset, Mrs. Winter?" Charley asked.

"Not very." She hesitated. "Mr. Krieg wasn't exactly very . . . likable."

"You hated him?"

"Despised him, Sergeant Deacon."

"Why did you despise him? What kind of dealings did you have with him?"

"Indirect relations. On the phone, when I tried to get some donations from him for the organizations I'm connected with. A man that wealthy who wouldn't give one penny? For anything? Everyone on the boards of these organizations despised him."

"Like . . ." Charley paused, and I actually heard his notebook pages rustling through the wall. "Mrs. Benson, and Mrs. Lang? Did they despise him?"

"Probably."

"Why?"

"Same reason I did. A man like that would rather give a hundred dollars to a maître d' to impress some bimbo than one dollar to help a starving artist."

"Did you know anyone who really hated him?"

"Of course. Everyone he ever came into contact with, most likely."

"Of the people at the chapel today, I mean."

"I only knew, closely, a few of the guests, but I would imagine that at least half the people there had good reason to hate him."

"Give me the names of the people you knew personally who hated him."

"Can't; hearsay and rumor." Even though I know she owns, and runs, a big business, this was a side of Lolly I'd never seen.

Charley drew a deep breath. "Then give me the names of all the people who'd been injured by Karl Krieg, in one way or another, about which you have knowledge."

"Sure, you and your four associates, then . . ."

"We're members of the police department! I never even met Mr. Krieg."

"Your job, Sergeant Deacon, is to protect the mayor from harm, and you've allowed Krieg to hurt the mayor politically. Put your own names down in your notebook, because if I am questioned by anyone else, I will make sure to mention that I told you what I told you."

Deacon sighed and, I presumed, wrote the five names into his book, because Lolly said, "Good work."

"Now I'll add the mayor's name," Charley told her, "since you told me Krieg had hurt the mayor. And your name too, since you're the mayor's friend and are hurt by anything that hurts the mayor."

Obviously he was thinking that two could play at this game.

"Then put down Mrs. Krieg," Lolly returned. "Guaranteed she hated him; any woman would."

There was a moment of silence, and I assumed Charley was busy writing.

"And Mr. and Mrs. Benson," Lolly instructed, "and Mr. and Mrs. Lang, and—"

"Would that be Mr. Kenneth Lang, the gentleman you were baby-sitting?"

"Not quite baby-sitting; Mr. Lang is a grown man. Actually, I wanted to make sure the father of the groom wouldn't drink too much."

"Is he a heavy drinker? What does he do when he gets drunk? Gets angry? Looks for a fight? What?"

"I don't think he's a heavy drinker, but people do tend to over-indulge at wedding receptions."

"Were you with him every moment of the time?" Charley pressed on.

"From about fifteen minutes before the ceremony began until maybe two or three minutes before we took our seats."

"About people who hated Mr. Krieg—are you forgetting Mr. Moshe Gur?" Charley prodded. "And maybe Mrs. Ruth Gur?"

"From what I know of him, Mr. Gur is a highly moral person; not the kind of person who would kill—"

"I didn't ask who the murderer was, Mrs. Winter; I asked who had been injured by the deceased."

"In that case, I suppose you could include them, though from what I know about them, I'm sure that—"

"That's my decision to make, Mrs. Winter," Charley said, all business. "I also noted a tall, gray-haired man who clearly didn't like Mr. Krieg. Who was he?"

"I didn't see him and I don't know anyone like that," Lolly said.

I knew who he meant: Frank Mardin.

But I wasn't about to stick my head in the door and tell Charley that.

"Okay," Charley said, and I heard the sound of a chair scraping against the tile floor. "Let's go to the Plaza. I'll see who else I can talk to there."

"It's very bad form," Lolly said, "to harass people at a wedding, and some of the guests are very important people."

"I know," Charley said firmly, "but, unfortunately, it's my job. And I'm going to do it right."

I wondered, once more, if he was seeing himself back in uniform, giving out parking tickets to tourists from New Jersey.

FIVE

Charley had arranged for someone to intercept Donna Krieg and inform her of her husband's death before we got to the Plaza.

By the time we arrived at the Terrace Room, the widow had already been escorted to her Park Avenue duplex by two NYPD detectives, and the place was abuzz with rumors.

Word had leaked out that Karl Krieg had been found dead at the chapel, though the news that it had been a grisly murder hadn't yet reached the guests.

"What's going on, Ed?" Moshe Gur asked, coming right over to me and Lolly a few minutes after we walked into the reception.

Ruth, at his side, looked slightly pale, and her pretty brown eyes showed concern.

"It's Karl Krieg," I told them. "He's dead."

"We heard that already. But what happened?"

I shrugged, having agreed, on the way over in the limo, that Lolly and I wouldn't spill any details at the reception.

I noted with some degree of relief that the curiosity on Moshe's face seemed genuine. I told myself that it wasn't that I had actually been suspicious of him . . .

But somehow, I couldn't seem to shake the memory of his earlier hostility toward Krieg.

"Ed, Lolly," Bevvy Benson called, pushing her way through the crowd at the edge of the dance floor. She looked distraught. "I just heard the news. Isn't it terrible about Karl?"

Lolly gave her a look that suggested we all knew there had been no love lost between Bevvy and Krieg.

Still, I had to admit that the woman did look genuinely upset. But then again, who wouldn't, when a guest at their daughter's wedding ceremony hadn't made it to the reception alive?

"Mrs. Benson?" Charley Deacon materialized at her elbow. "Can I speak with you for a few moments, please?"

"Can it wait?" Beverly asked, swiftly recovering her composure and turning calmly to him. "You know that I *am* the mother of the bride, and I have several hundred guests to attend to."

"I'm afraid it can't wait," Charley said, and put a hand on her arm. "Please come with me."

I saw Moshe and Ruth exchange a glance as he led Bevvy away.

Moshe turned to me. "Ed, he doesn't think that she—"

"Don't be ridiculous," Lolly cut in. "Bevvy isn't a suspect any more than the rest of us are."

"So Krieg *was* murdered?" Moshe asked.

Lolly looked at me.

Reluctantly, I nodded. "But it would be better if you didn't let the word out here," I cautioned Moshe and Ruth. "You wouldn't want to frighten everyone, or ruin the night for Aileen and Alan."

"No, we wouldn't want to do that," Moshe murmured, glancing toward the dance floor, where the happy bride and groom were waltzing to an old Sinatra tune.

I didn't tell Moshe that he, too, would undoubtedly be questioned by detectives before the affair was over.

Speculation about Krieg's death was the mainstay of conversation among the guests for the rest of the evening. Even so, the orchestra played and the drinks flowed.

And while there wasn't exactly a replay of the "Ding! Dong! The Witch is Dead" scene from *The Wizard of Oz,* no one at the wedding seemed to be particularly in mourning.

This was a murder investigation, and even the murder of a bastard like Karl Krieg must be investigated thoroughly and honestly.

Charley and his men made the rounds among the guests, questioning just about everyone at the reception, and making it pretty obvious that Krieg hadn't dropped dead of a heart attack.

After the last drop of champagne had evaporated and the orchestra had played its final number, Lolly and I decided to go to her condo, as she'd already given her staff the night off and we could talk privately there.

"You know what?" I asked as we stepped off the elevator into the high-ceilinged foyer of her apartment. "I'm starved."

"How could you be? That wedding reception was loaded with food."

"I know, but after what happened with Krieg, I wasn't in the mood to eat much. Now, all of the sudden, I feel like I could," I said hopefully.

Lolly sighed and started toward the kitchen, waving at me to follow. "Come on, I'll see what I can come up with. I'm actually kind of hungry myself."

Lolly's kitchen, in keeping with the rest of her place, is one of those all-modern, stainless steel and glass affairs that you see in *Metropolitan Home* magazine. The cupboards and refrigerators are generally fully stocked.

Meanwhile, Lolly, as I was well aware when I suggested a snack, is something of a gourmet cook when she wants to be.

I sat at the kitchen table making small talk while she cracked eggs expertly with one hand into a large mixing bowl, then slaved over a hot Gruyère omelette, working to get the outside evenly solid while leaving the center a bit liquid, just the way I like it.

"So why were you baby-sitting Ken Lang?" I asked finally, bored with idle chatter about the wedding guests and the food at the reception and the bride and groom.

Lolly flipped the pan to roll up the omelette, let it rest there a moment, then tilted the pan to slide the finished masterpiece onto a warmed plate.

"Let's wait to get into that until after we've eaten. I don't want to lose my appetite again." She put the plate in front of me, then turned back to the mixing bowl where her portion of the beaten eggs was waiting.

A tantalizing aroma wafted up to my nostrils and I obliged without argument, picking up my fork and digging in. When I had finished the omelette, I showed my appreciation by wiping my plate clean with a chunk of the baguette Lolly had warmed in the oven.

When Lolly had finished too, she said, "How about some coffee?"

Though Lolly makes a mean omelette, I happen to know that her coffee-brewing skills don't hold a candle to mine.

"I'll make it," I offered, "provided we can talk at the same time."

"Fine." She put her stocking feet up on a chair, leaned back, and pointed. "The coffee's up there."

I went to the cupboard she'd indicated, pulled out a likely canister, and sniffed the contents, then peered inside.

"Not Martinson's?" I asked, disappointed.

Lolly rolled her eyes. "No, but this happens to be a fine imported Swedish blend. Try it, I guarantee that you'll like it."

I made a mental note to teach Lolly what I'd taught Rosemary about making coffee. But not tonight. I didn't want any more distractions.

As I set about following the steps of my foolproof recipe, I told her, "Okay, start talking. I have to know about Ken Lang."

"Why?"

"Because even though Charley says I'm not a suspect, the questions he was asking made me a little nervous."

"What kind of questions did he ask?"

"Nothing that was outright incriminating, but still . . . It's well-known that I didn't like Krieg, and I was one of the people close to where he was killed—it was in an alcove at the back of the chapel. If they don't find the real killer, there'll always be the suspicion in the minds of the people—and in most of the newspapers—that I was involved."

I didn't want to act worried, but I didn't feel fully confident either.

"You don't actually think you could lose the next election if the killer isn't caught?"

"Easily."

Now that the coffee was brewing, I leaned against the counter, folded my arms across my chest, and looked at her. "Politics is the art of the possible, which means you have to do what you have to do to get done what you gotta get done."

"If you're trying to confuse me, you're doing a good job." She regarded me suspiciously. "What are you getting at? You're not going to do anything unethical, are you?"

"Of course not. But what do you do if there's a conflict between two ethical actions?"

"What do you mean?"

"I mean, what if I saw some people who, I'm sure, couldn't be murderers, standing near the back wall of the chapel the way I was?"

Lolly's eyes narrowed. "What if you did?"

"Remember when I phoned the police commissioner from the limo?"

"I didn't know who you called and I didn't understand a word you were saying."

"Though I didn't use the exact words, I tried to convince the commissioner there was nothing to be gained by grabbing these people for questioning tonight."

"Who were these people," she asked warily, "the ones who were standing near the back wall?"

"I'll tell you in a minute. Anyway, it didn't work. They were all interrogated at the reception. What I'm trying to say is, what you're keeping from me, the police will get from their investigation anyway. This is something they're good at."

"And if I tell you about Ken Lang?"

"If I can prove he's the killer, I'll turn him over to the police."

"And if you can't prove he's the killer?"

"I'll figure out who is. When I was a lawyer, I saved Vinnie Lobosco—"

"Not the guy who had more parking violations than the rest of the world put together?"

"One and the same. He's paying them off weekly and I hope he lives long enough to finish. Anyway, he was being tried for murder two. I was a practicing lawyer then, and I saved Vinnie by figuring out who the real killer was, and there were hundreds of possibilities. Here there are only a few; a piece of cake. Now talk."

Lolly seemed to be thinking it over. "If I help you, Ed, then the killer, who's probably a nice person, goes to jail, most likely for life. Keep in mind that the victim here is a lousy slimeball who should've been murdered long ago."

"And you should keep in mind that *I* saw the body. Anyone who did what someone did to Karl Krieg couldn't be *that* nice a person," I told her.

She shrugged. "Good point, but . . ."

"Come on, Lolly."

"All right, I'll help you. You promise to find the real killer, no matter what . . . right?"

"That's the whole point," I explained patiently. "Now can we get back to Ken Lang?"

"All right, all right." She took a deep breath, and announced, "Ken had once said that he was going to kill Karl Krieg." She waited for my reaction.

"That's the big secret? There must be a thousand people in New York who've said the same thing."

"They weren't all in the chapel."

"True, but . . ." I shrugged. "Okay, that's a good start. Ken Lang is suspect number one. What about Bevvy?"

"What about her? She recently had a big fight with Krieg, but knowing Bevvy, I'm sure she wouldn't do anything as crude as sticking a knife into Krieg."

"Still, she did have a motive."

"I suppose, if you can call it that."

"I can. Now we're getting someplace," I said, turning to see if the coffee was done. It was. "Cups?" I asked Lolly.

"Third cupboard over, on the left."

I found two heavy, hand-painted Italian porcelain mugs, filled them, and set them on the table.

Lolly, I knew, took her coffee black and unsweetened, just as I do.

I sat across from her again.

"Ken Lang and Bevvy," she said, reaching for her coffee, and shook her head. "I just don't see either of them as the killer."

"That doesn't mean one of them isn't guilty."

"Fine. Who else?"

I hated to say it, but I had no choice. "I guess we might as well add Moshe Gur to the list. I'm sure he couldn't bring himself to kill anyone, but who knows what evil lurks in the hearts of men?"

"Or women. How about Donna Krieg?"

"Definitely a suspect," I agreed, lifting my steaming mug and taking a cautious sip. It wasn't bad, considering it wasn't my usual brand. "Anyone close to Krieg is probably going to be a suspect. After all . . ."

"To know him was to hate him," Lolly supplied.

I nodded. "Exactly. There's Frank Mardin, too. He's a tall, sort of gray-haired man."

Lolly nodded recognition. "I saw him around. His wife is short and gray-haired?"

"That's her. Joan Mardin."

"What's she like?"

"She's very nice, as far as I know. Tough, but nice. He's not bad, but he's no softy, either. They're developers. Good firm. Do their own engineering and architecture. They have to hate Krieg, too, and Frank Mardin was definitely near the rear wall at the time of the murder."

"How about his wife?"

"She had a seat for the ceremony—I remember seeing her somewhere near the front."

"Okay," Lolly said, "I can't think think of anyone else. Can you?"

"Nope; that's it. Five possible murderers."

"Six," Lolly said, "counting yourself."

"Very funny."

"You know you're innocent, and I know you're innocent, but as you pointed out earlier, Ed, the press won't know and the voters won't know."

We looked at each other for a long time.

Then I sipped my coffee and said, "I'm going to solve this, Lolly. I'm going to stay one step ahead of Charley and the other detectives. I'm going to find out who killed Karl Krieg, and I'm going to find out ASAP."

She nodded. "I have only one more thing to say to you."

"What's that?"

"Good luck. You're going to need it."

SIX

I wasn't surprised to discover, the next morning, that Charley Deacon and the rest of my usual Gang had been replaced with five new bodyguards from the NYPD.

One of them, Marv Kozlowski, who had guarded me on occasion before, told me that Charley and the others were temporarily working on another assignment. He didn't say it, but they were obviously wrapped up in the investigation into Karl Krieg's murder.

And so, it seemed, was the rest of the city.

I'd risen earlier than usual—despite the fact that I hadn't returned home from Lolly's until well after midnight—and gone out to fetch all the morning papers.

As I had anticipated, Karl Krieg's murder was front-page news. His fleshy, beady-eyed face, captured in various paparazzi shots taken over the years, stared out at me from the cover of every local tabloid.

Most of the newspaper accounts were sketchy, but all of them mentioned that I had been questioned, and that the police weren't ruling out any suspects yet. It wasn't as if anyone was outright hinting that I might have something to do with Krieg's murder, but my obvious link to this scandal didn't exactly bode well for my upcoming campaign.

I had the feeling this was going to be a long day.

This time, after the limo driver had gone past the guardhouse and ten-foot security wall that surrounds the mansion, he headed across town on East Eighty-sixth, then went through the park and down the west side until we reached midtown. My bodyguards like to take a different route to City Hall every day, to foil would-be assassins.

We drove down Seventh Avenue past Macy's, where enormous, bright-colored banners advertised their annual Spring Flower Show, and then over to Broadway.

The weather had done an about-face over the weekend; the city was gray and windy and drizzly this morning. Pedestrians scurried along the sidewalks, most of them dressed in somber-colored raincoats, their heads and shoulders obscured by umbrellas.

When we reached the City Hall parking lot, I wasn't the least bit surprised to see several members of the press camped out on the front steps that lead to the portico. As soon as they spotted the limo, they came sloshing over, cameras, microphones, and notebooks poised. Some were already shouting as they jostled for position outside the car.

Marv sighed and shook his head. "Look at them, splashing around out there and quacking like a bunch of ducks."

I rolled my eyes, sighed, and stepped out of the backseat.

Marv promptly opened an umbrella and stood behind me, holding it over my head.

"Mr. Mayor . . ."

"Mr. Mayor . . ."

"Mr. Mayor . . ."

The reporters surrounded me, and I held up a hand as if to fend them off. "I'm not going to say a word," I said firmly, "till you take those mikes out of my face."

The reporters obliged by pulling back slightly.

One of them, who I recognized as being from a suburban tabloid, asked, "What do you know about the murder in the City Hall chapel?"

"What do *I* know? Nothing. Why don't you ask the police commissioner? That's his job."

"He's not talking yet," another reporter said. "How could you know nothing when you were right there?"

"What's the name of the reporter who's pressing against your back?" I asked.

No answer; he didn't even turn around.

"That's how I don't know anything about the murder. The killer forgot to tell me to watch while he was doing it."

"So you think the killer was a man?" another reporter asked.

I sighed heavily. "That was a generic 'he.' About fifty percent of the people in the chapel were women, so there is a fifty percent possibility that the killer could have been a woman, mathematically speaking."

Another reporter chimed in. "Isn't it true that everyone in the chapel at the time of the murder was a friend of yours?"

"Absolutely untrue," I said. "One of the bartenders looked somewhat unfamiliar to me."

With that, I shoved my way toward the door, flanked by Marv and the other detectives.

We left the throng of reporters behind just as the skies opened up with an ominous bang and the rain started pouring down in earnest, drenching them.

The last person I expected to see waiting outside my office when I returned from a lunch meeting at my favorite restaurant in Little Italy was Bevvy Benson.

But there she was, perched on a bench looking quite dry and elegant in her black Burberry raincoat and charcoal-colored Chanel suit. She stood and came toward me, a cloud of expensive floral perfume wafting around her.

Behind her, Rosemary Larkin flashed me an apologetic look.

"Ed, how are you?"

"Fine, Bevvy. What can I do for you?"

"I was doing some work in the Municipal Building," Bevvy said in her usual straightforward way, "which is a two-minute walk from here, and I thought it might be to your benefit as well as mine if I dropped in."

"Oh?" I removed my own beige trench coat, which was soaked from the few steps I'd taken from the restaurant to the car, and gestured toward my closed door. "Why don't you step into my office."

"I'd be glad to."

Rosemary cleared her throat meaningfully, and I glanced at her.

"The school superintendent is waiting in the small conference room for your two o'clock meeting," she informed me.

"Tell him I'll be with him momentarily, would you?" I instructed, then ushered Bevvy into my office and closed the door firmly behind me.

I took her coat, hung it in the corner closet beside my own, and waved her to sit down.

She did, then leaned forward and clasped her hands on the glass top of my prized La Guardia desk.

As soon as I'd taken my place behind it, she plunged right in. "I hope you're willing to listen to reason, Ed."

I blinked. "I'm always willing to listen to reason, Bevvy. You know that about me. Obviously, you have something important to discuss. Do you want me to call Rosemary in to take notes?"

"This isn't about business. I know what you're thinking, but believe me, I'm not here to talk about the Muni Yard Project; I don't take advantage of friendship to push business deals."

"If it's about Lolly . . ."

"It's about Lolly, but not the way you think. Tell me something, Ed; if you were sent to prison for murder tomorrow, you think the city wouldn't survive?"

"It would survive, but how well?" I responded promptly. "You want to check out the way the city fared under some of our past mayors? It might open your eyes. And what's this about being sent to prison for murder?"

"That's what I came to talk to you about. Lolly tried to interrogate me today. She acted as though she was just making conversation, but I knew better. Lolly may be the smartest super-beautiful woman in the universe, but when it comes to second place beauties like me, she's not even in the running for practical shrewdness."

"Lolly happens to be exceptionally smart," I informed Bevvy, "and it'll be to everyone's benefit if she solves this case, whether by getting information from you or by any other means. As for me . . . You know how I can put apparently unconnected elements together to make a coherent pattern. I'm going to solve this crime, and fast. Or Lolly will. Or we both will, together."

"It better be fast, Ed, because if it hangs around too much longer, there are lots of columnists in this town who are very good at putting a story together out of two whispers and an innuendo. Like 'What well-known mayor has been accused of delaying an important murder investigation in which he and several of his friends may have been involved?' "

" 'Delaying'? Don't be silly, Bev; the murder was yesterday and already Lolly is working on it. I can't, not during working hours."

"Then I'll do your part for you," Bevvy said, and shifted in her seat. "The murder had to take place between the time the chairs were taken from the alcoves and the time they were put back or, rather, partly put back. A matter of about twenty minutes, right?"

"Wrong." Very few people know how precisely and accurately I watch everything around me. "The window of opportunity was open only about fifteen minutes, probably less, ending at the time the last guest left, just before the caterer's crew started to put the chairs back. Don't forget, the whole wedding ceremony took less than ten minutes."

"I stand corrected," Bevvy said. "Very impressive, Ed."

"Thank you."

"As one of the last people to leave, I was watching everything very carefully."

"I'm sure you did."

"I saw that as soon as almost all of the guests had left, the caterers started clearing away the unused food and drink, cleaning up, dumping the organic garbage into a can, bagging the used napkins, putting the plastics into another bag—all very ecologically correct—pouring the partly finished drinks into a barrel, closing the bar, and getting ready to move out. They moved very quickly and efficiently. Some were even putting back chairs while the others were wrapping up."

"So you openly admit you were one of the last to leave," I told Bevvy. "And everyone knows you had a falling-out with Karl Krieg. Which means that you're a prime suspect."

"Absolutely true, Ed"—she smiled confidently—"but remind me of something; how did I get the dagger past the metal detectors and into the chapel? And how did I carry it around for an hour in the form-fitting dress I was wearing? And why should I spoil my only daughter's wedding by having a murder as the entertainment?"

"You got me," I said in a noncommittal tone.

"And," Bevvy continued, "since I know Karl Krieg quite well, couldn't I have waited a few more days and met him in some place where I could kill him in a safe way that would never be connected to me? And least importantly, he was going to give me over two million dollars today. Wouldn't it have saved me some time, trouble, and money to take the two million and kill him next week instead of having to sue his estate?"

I thought for a moment, then said, "Do you have any evidence of that two-million-dollar deal?"

Bevvy hesitated. "I don't usually do it, but Krieg was being such a bastard that . . ."

When she paused again, I prodded, "Such a bastard that what?"

She sighed. "I taped my last phone call to him, for good reason, so if I do have to sue his estate to get my money, I have the evidence that he promised to pay what he owed me today. At my bank."

Now here was a provocative development. I leaned forward and steepled my fingers on the desk top. "I'd like to hear that tape," I told Bevvy.

"If you want to hear it, you have to bring Lolly with you; I need a witness."

"I can't go to your office now; it'll look like— And we can't listen to it here."

"Lolly's apartment or mine, Ed. Seven o'clock tomorrow."

"Lolly's."

"Fine."

Bevvy and I exchanged a long look.

"Ed, you don't still suspect me, do you?" she finally asked. "I just told you a million reasons why I wouldn't—*couldn't*—have done it."

Being a lawyer, I don't take things said by suspects as the absolute truth. "What you say makes sense, but so will every argument by someone who's trying to save his neck. I'll think about it and talk to you again."

"Let me give you a better scenario," Bevvy said. "Who was the last guest left?"

"I didn't notice," I said.

"Sure you did; it was you."

"I wasn't a guest; I performed the ceremony."

She gave me a level look.

"Okay," I gave in, "I was the last guest left."

"Who was practically alone in the chapel before the cleanup started? Who disliked—we all know that means hated—Karl Krieg? Who is important enough to lure Krieg into the alcove, and strong enough to push the fat little man into the alcove if necessary?"

"There was no time," I objected.

"The way I figure it, once he's in the alcove, the killer puts the right hand over Krieg's mouth in case he makes a sound, as the left hand stabs him. I could do it in three seconds. You could do it in two. And how did the dagger get into the chapel, past the metal detectors?"

"I have no idea. So far."

"Who was the only guest who didn't go through the metal detector? And I don't mean Lolly."

"Are you accusing me"—I was really indignant—"of committing murder?"

I was aware of Fiorello La Guardia staring down at me over Bevvy's shoulder from a portrait on the wall opposite my desk. I wondered what he would think of a mayor who found himself considered a prime suspect in a murder case.

"Of course I'm not accusing you of committing murder," Bevvy said. "Although you just about accused me a few minutes ago. I was only showing you how easy it is, in those circumstances, to make a half-assed case against any one of my friends. What I'm suggesting is that you leave the detecting to the police."

"The police are not at their best in a case like this; their ways of working are quite different. This case requires analysis and synthesis, at which I'm really expert. I'm also practical: I know how this world works and how to get things done. I'm an attorney as well as the mayor and, I assure you, I will crack this case. And soon. Very soon."

It was a promise to old Fiorello as well as to her.

"Sure you will," said Bevvy, getting up. "Just leave my friends alone. And that goes for my new in-laws too."

"I don't play favorites," I said.

"I do," she informed me crisply.

SEVEN

Rosemary came into my office just before six o'clock, looking flustered, which was rare.

Sensing that something was up, I set aside the budget report I had been scanning. "What is it, Rosemary?"

"First, there's a message from Mrs. Winter."

That was good news. I'd been trying to reach Lolly all afternoon. We had decided, before we parted last night, to meet tonight to discuss the case.

"She's in the financial district on business," Rosemary said, "and she's finished with her work. She'll catch a cab and meet you at the front entrance in fifteen minutes."

"Okay, I'll be there. What else?"

There was a pause. Rosemary looked down and ran the toe of her sensible black pump along a groove in the carpet. Finally, she glanced up and said, "It's about the murder."

"What about it? You have a theory you want to run by me, like everyone else I've come across today has?"

"A theory? Only this—that it took a woman's brains."

"How do you know?"

"The knife. It's not a stabbing knife, it's a slipping-in-smoothly knife that didn't need muscles, just brains."

"How do you know what it was? Even I don't know and I'm

supposed to be briefed up to the minute on everything that happens in this city.''

She glanced over her shoulder at the door she'd closed behind her, as though someone might be eavesdropping.

Then she cleared her throat and said mysteriously and so quietly I had to lean forward just to hear her, "I've got connections.''

I raised a brow. "What kind of connections?''

"On your way to the front door to meet Mrs. Winter, stop by my desk. There'll be a big brown envelope in the top middle drawer.'' She paused for effect. "It'll be marked 'Police Department Property—Do Not Remove.' ''

I stared into her unblinking gray eyes. "You actually did something illegal, Rosemary?''

"Of course not. *I* didn't remove it.''

"Who did?''

She shrugged. "I have—''

"I know, I know. You have connections. But this case is hot. Someone has to know the envelope is missing, Rosemary.''

"All the information is a duplicate, so they'll never know.''

"But even to have it . . .''

"All right, if you're not interested . . .''

"Maybe I should just take a fast look at it,'' I said quickly, "on the way home. After all, the crime took place on my turf.''

"That's right, and you're one of the prime suspects, so you had better figure this one out fast. Why do you think I got it for you? It cost me an enormous favor, too—one that I was saving for something really important.''

"Meaning I'm not really important? And I'm considered a *prime* suspect, huh? Where did you hear that? From the police?''

"I never reveal my sources and you better not even ask who they are; they could be as useful to you in the future as they were in the past, provided it wasn't you who killed the fat little bastard.''

I didn't know whether I was taken aback more by her implication, or by the un–Rosemary-like language. I echoed, "Provided I . . . ? *Provided?*''

"Oh, come on, Mayor, you should be flattered that I might think you could have—not that I think you *did.* ''

"*Flattered?* Flattered that I could be a murderer? That's ridiculous!"

"Flattered that I think you have the guts to do it and the brains to commit a perfect crime. Politicians today kill with their tongues, and you're really expert at that, but in the good old days they knew how to really shut up a rival."

"Krieg was no rival and . . . What good old days? Nothing like what you're hinting at ever happened in New York."

"Who said New York? I meant Rome. The *real* Rome that ran the whole known world in those days. That's when a politician had to watch what he said and to whom. So anytime you're ready to start wearing a toga, Boss, I'm with you all the way. And don't forget, you have five bodyguards and nobody else in the administration has any."

"Thanks for the offer, Rosemary; it's very comforting to know you'll be on my side when comes the revolution."

She looked pleased.

"Meanwhile," I went on, "call my bodyguards and tell them that I won't be riding with them after work, but that they'll be bracketing me. Then call Vinnie and tell him to pick up Mrs. Winter and me here right away. Not *him*—make that very clear—any one of his regular drivers, but not him."

"Are you crazy? Vinnie Lobosco? In rush hour traffic?"

"I told you to get one of his drivers, not him."

"When it comes to you, he doesn't listen."

She had a point. Oh, well.

"Don't worry," I told her, "even if he insists on driving. Awhile back, Charley figured out a technique to use in situations like this. The front car will make Vinnie a tailgater in reverse by keeping its rear bumper practically touching my front bumper. This will slow Vinnie down to the point where the official limo can tailgate him, be right up Vinnie's tailpipe. There's no way he can even speed, much less do whatever he's in the mood for today."

"Why don't you get rid of Vinnie altogether? It's not like he'd starve; he could make a fortune in a demolition derby."

"I can't. Not only would he give his life for me, I saved his life once. If you save a man, according to an ancient Chinese proverb, you're responsible for him for the rest of his life."

"But Vinnie's not Chinese. Besides, knowing this—and his driving record—why did you save his life?"

"I had to. I was his lawyer and he'd been falsely accused of murder."

"With a car, no doubt."

"With a gun. I examined the clues and interrogated people and put everything in its logical order and found the real killer. Just like I'm going to find out who killed Karl Krieg."

"If you're serious, Boss, maybe you should spend a little less time on the municipal details and a little more time on detecting."

"I have to do my job; the detecting I'll do when I can. Now tell me something. Why did you get the information on the murder weapon?"

"I really hate the idea of breaking in a new mayor," she said, and I figured that was probably a big part of the truth.

Still, I knew Rosemary and I had a real bond after all these years, one that went beyond a mere professional relationship.

"I'll see if I can pick up any more info," she offered. "Meanwhile, I'll call Vinnie. Mrs. Winter should be here by now and you're late already, even if you run."

I stood and tucked the budget report into my briefcase. "Thanks for everything, Rosemary."

"No problem. Just make sure that envelope's back on my desk by nine o'clock tomorrow morning."

"Where's Charley?" Lolly asked when I met her downstairs. "And the other regulars?"

"Special assignment," I said, and she nodded knowingly. "Listen, we're going to take my limo."

"Ohmygod," Lolly said. "With Vinnie?"

"Don't worry, the front car and the limo are under orders to keep us locked in, and at this time of day there's no way anyone can go faster than a crawl."

"He still scares me."

"So do what he does—close your eyes."

Lolly flinched. "Why can't we take a taxi or a different private limo?"

"I don't want to make anyone suspicious. Why would we take a private limo when we have the official limo, with bodyguards, at our disposal? With Vinnie, I can always say I like the way he drives, or that we're friends."

"And you expect anyone to believe that?"

I shrugged. "I'm not allowed to be eccentric? Or to try to help a fellow human being make a living?"

"Vinnie owns at least twenty limos. What's the real reason?"

I looked around carefully. "Secrecy," I said, without moving my lips. "I have, in my briefcase, the police file on the murder weapon."

Lolly gasped. "Is that legal?"

"I'd have to ask the corporation counsel, and he's out of town."

I heard screeching tires and an engine gunning and glanced out the door at the rain-slicked street just in time to see a big, vintage, tail-finned Cadillac pull up fast. Its front wheels mounted the first two steps of the City Hall stairs and scattered a crowd of pedestrians.

"Your chariot," I said with a sweep of my arm, and Lolly rolled her eyes.

We stepped outside. It was no longer raining, but everything was damp and misty.

Vinnie Lobosco stuck his slick-haired head out of the side window and yelled, "Twelve minutes and twenty-eight seconds."

"Fantastic," I called. "Now pull back so we can get in, please."

The wheels squealed as Vinnie pulled back with the accelerator floored, then the tires screamed as Vinnie hit the brakes so he could stop just before knocking down the fence around City Hall Park. I held up my hand to keep Vinnie from coming back toward us, then Lolly and I walked toward the car.

A young reporter suddenly materialized. "Mr. Mayor, are you aware of any more developments in the Krieg murder case?"

"No," I said simply, still walking.

"But you are aware that both you and Mrs. Winter are suspects?" another reporter asked, dogging our heels.

I didn't bother to respond to that, but out of the corner of my eye, I saw Lolly's jaw drop slightly.

The first reporter held his mike three inches from Lolly's face, and asked, "Did you do it, Mrs. Winter?"

"Of course I didn't."

"Mr. Mayor, do you have any information on who *did* do it?"

"Absolutely not," I said. "Do you?"

He looked taken aback.

"Well, keep me posted," I told him, "if you hear anything new. Okay?"

We had reached Vinnie's car and got into the backseat as my bodyguards jumped into the other two waiting vehicles. Once we were settled inside, Lolly said, "I hate invasions of my person and my privacy. How do you put up with this day after day?"

"Goes with the territory," I said. "And if you ask me, it's a small price to pay in exchange for being mayor of the greatest city in the world."

Vinnie picked up the voice tube. "Where to, Mr. Mayor?"

"Mrs. Winter's apartment," I said, using my end of the tube. "It's on—"

"I know where it is. I drove you there for that big New Year's bash, remember?"

I remembered, all right. It had been icy that night, and I'd felt lucky to make it to the new year alive.

"You know, come to think of it, it's been three months since you called me, Mr. Mayor," Vinnie said. "I didn't do nothing wrong, did I?"

"Of course not. I have to ride in the official car almost all of the time, Vinnie. The bodyguards get nervous."

"Jerks. Nobody'd have the guts to take a shot at you when I'm driving. I'd flatten 'em out like pancakes."

"I know that," I said, "but the Police Department has regulations and even I have to follow them. You can concentrate on driving now; the way the bodyguard cars are hugging us front and back, you're going to need both hands."

We both hung up our tubes.

"Why my place?" Lolly asked.

"Privacy," I said simply.

I unsnapped my briefcase and took out the police envelope. "This is the official information about the murder weapon."

She gasped. "How did you get your hands on it?"

"I have connections," I said smugly, recycling Rosemary's line.

I opened the flap and slid the contents out into the open brief-case.

There was a handful of papers and photocopies of official forms, and several glossy eight-by-ten color photos of the murder weapon, one with the paper handle and the blood still on it, the others of different views of the bloody, simple metal dagger, an odd sort of knife. All the photos had a ruler in the picture to show the weapon's dimensions.

"We can't really analyze this in a moving car," Lolly said, "especially if I have to keep closing my eyes and digging in my heels and grabbing for the strap every time Vinnie makes a turn. Let's wait till we get to my place."

I didn't want to wait. The phrase "prime suspect" kept ringing in my ears. The sooner I solved this case, the better.

There was a screech as Vinnie slammed on the brakes to avoid ramming into the car in front of us, and Lolly and I flew forward despite our seat belts. I had to grab the contents of the folder to keep them from spilling all over the floor of the car.

"You're right," I told her, reluctantly putting the papers back into the envelope. "We'll wait."

As soon as we got into the apartment, Lolly kicked off her shoes. "I hate high heels," she said, "but the idiots who had the luck to fall into high-ranking jobs in money companies expect it. I'm going to change my clothes. I'll be back in a few minutes."

"Oh, sure you will." I held up the briefcase. "But don't worry. I have plenty to keep me occupied while you're gone."

"What about dinner?"

"We can send out for some Szechuan hot stuff later. Or maybe two dozen mixed *dim sum,* pot luck, all fried, no steamed."

"Sounds good, but no duck feet, no sea cucumber, no fish lips, and no anything I don't usually eat. Make yourself comfortable in the living room for a few minutes. And for heaven's sake, Ed, why don't you drink something relaxing; you look tense."

"That's because I'm uncomfortable as long as this stuff is in my possession." I went into the living room and poured myself a small brandy.

I knew, from experience, that Lolly wouldn't be a few minutes.

I settled down to start going over the material in the file so that I would be prepared to bounce ideas off of Lolly when she got back.

It always helps me to think out loud. Besides, I knew Lolly wouldn't feel the need to agree with me because I was the mayor.

When she finally came back, she was wearing a fuzzy white robe and slippers. She had clearly taken a shower, not just changed her clothes. Her hair was tied back loosely and her face was glowing, with not a drop of makeup for a change.

"How many brandies have you lapped up while I wasn't watching?" she asked, eyeing me as she sat down next to me on the white damask couch. "We have work to do, or have you forgotten?"

"Just one," I said. "Actually not even a whole drink. I've been reading through these reports, and I need to have my wits about me. And by the way, before I forget, you and I are going to interrogate Bevvy here tomorrow at seven."

"Bevvy? She didn't do it. I was going to mention earlier that I already talked to her today—not that I suspected her in the first place."

"Look, Lolly, we have to check all the suspects thoroughly to clear them. And you're not the only one who talked to Bevvy today. She says she has a tape she wants us to hear."

"What tape?"

"A telephone conversation she had with Karl Krieg. She says it'll prove she's innocent."

"Bevvy and I have been friends since school. I know her inside and out. We roomed together. I know she didn't do it—she doesn't have to prove anything to me."

"Fair enough," I said. "Just listen to the tape and watch her face."

"Why do you need me on this?" Lolly asked. "I'm very knowledgeable about money and corporate affairs, administration, things like that. But I'm not a scientist or a detective or an expert on knives. So why me?"

"I have a very broad knowledge," I said, "of many areas that I picked up as a politician and as a lawyer. I know how to interrogate people and how to deduce solutions to problems from given facts and information. Vinnie Lobosco is a perfect example. Everything pointed to him as the killer, but I saw there were flaws in the DA's reasoning and, when I put my evidence in the right order, it was clear who the killer was. I'm going to do the same thing here."

"You haven't answered my question, Ed. Why me? I don't know anyone who'd let me even see the evidence in a case like this, much less want my opinion."

"Two views are important. You'll see, think, know things that I don't. Your interpretation of the facts, of what we both see, will be different from mine. You may notice something I miss."

Lolly smiled, obviously pleased at her role.

I spread out the pictures. "Keep your eyes on the photos as I describe them. If what I say varies from what you see, no matter how slightly, stop me immediately."

Lolly nodded and stared at the pictures.

"First photo," I said, "the murder weapon in place in the body of the victim, just below the sternum and slightly angled to the victim's left to penetrate the heart. The autopsy shows that the weapon was moved—quickly wiggled—from side to side and that the victim's heart was cut in several places."

I paused so that Lolly could absorb that grisly information.

"Approximately three inches of handle is visible," I went on, "the handle consisting of just a wad of papers, now partially soaked with blood. As an aside, when I first saw the body, the paper handle had only a little bit of blood on it. The report says that these papers are exactly like the cocktail napkins given out by the caterer. No fingerprints were obtained from the papers and no DNA separation has been made yet."

"Why would anyone use paper for a handle?" Lolly asked.

"Good point," I told her. "And beyond that, how would the killer know that paper was available? We heard Bevvy arguing with the woman in charge, acting as though she expected silver, china, crystal, and *cloth* napkins. Damask napkins."

"That's right, I remember," Lolly said, nodding.

"By the same reasoning, why go to the trouble of bringing in a knife when it could be expected that there would be lots of knives there? And if not there, certainly at the dinner at the Plaza? In fact, the Plaza would be the perfect place; almost a thousand people at the reception, lots of places for privacy, and you don't have to go through a metal detector. If you worked it right, it would be hours before the body was found."

"True. So what are you thinking?" Lolly asked.

"That this is beginning to look like a complicated case. Now let's examine the murder weapon. A piece of flexible steel about eight inches long, three-quarters of an inch wide, and an eighth inch thick. It has a point at one end and a squared end at the other. The edges and the point are very sharp, like a good knife, and there is a slight bend in the blade near the pointed end. A very unusual shape, almost like a ski."

"Why?"

"I would think that the bend is to make sure that when the killer stabbed Krieg, the point would penetrate the heart and not just go in straight and miss the heart. The sharpness at both sides is to slice the heart so that Krieg would die immediately."

I saw her wince before she said, "I have a question, Ed. The length of the knife. Is five inches long enough to hit the heart?"

"Absolutely, according to the report I just read. From that point of penetration, four inches would work. Even less, with a little care."

"Three inches is a very short handle," Lolly said. "So why not make the knife nine inches long rather than eight? I mean, this knife was obviously homemade; I don't think I could buy one like it anywhere. So why that length? And why that thickness and width? Wouldn't it have been surer to get one a little longer, a little wider, and a little thicker? With a handle you could hold?"

"Exactly," I said with a nod. "You could buy a proper dagger for stabbing people with in some schlock store near Eighth Avenue, where the clerk wouldn't remember you if you painted your nose purple."

"Unless you were the mayor," Lolly pointed out. "Or someone equally recognizable. Not that I suspect *you*, Ed."

I snorted.

"And how did the killer get that knife past the metal detector?" Lolly asked. "Was it broken or not working or something? Did the electricity go off for a few seconds?"

"No, it didn't." I sighed. "This isn't going to be easy. Nothing fits together."

"Well, one thing makes sense. The fact that Karl Krieg was murdered in the first place. The guy was a creep who deserved to be killed. You and I both know that half the people there wanted to kill him—probably including his wife—and would've if they could've figured out how."

"All our suspects are smart, Lolly. And didn't you once tell me that Bevvy Benson is the smartest woman you ever knew?"

She narrowed her eyes at me. "Only in a nice, helpful way."

I shrugged. "We'll find out tomorrow, won't we?"

———— EIGHT

I didn't get very much sleep Monday night. I
kept thinking of new details I needed to check into regarding the
case. Every time something occurred to me, I got out of bed,
turned on the light, and jotted a note on the yellow legal pad I had
placed on my nightstand for just that purpose. I do that whenever
something weighty is on my mind.

Tuesday morning, bleary-eyed even after three cups of coffee
and my usual grapefruit, I tucked the list of notes into my briefcase, along with the manila envelope I had to return to Rosemary.

As soon as I opened the door of my official limousine, I saw that
Charley was back on the job—but only Charley, which was odd.
The other regulars were still, apparently, otherwise occupied.

"Morning, Mayor," Charley said as I climbed into the backseat
next to him. "How've you been?"

"How do you think?" I retorted.

I made sure the briefcase with the police files in it was tightly
latched as I placed it on the floor at my feet.

"Did you see this morning's papers?" I asked Charley.

"What about them?"

"One of the tabloids ran a piece on the murder under the head-
line, 'Koch a Killer?' "

Charley shifted uncomfortably as the limo driver pulled onto
East Eighty-sixth Street. "Yeah, I saw it."

"Charley, *you* know I didn't kill Krieg"— at least, I hoped he
knew that—"and *I* know I didn't kill Krieg, but until the real murderer is caught, the people of this city aren't going to know it. The
press is going to have a field day with this, regardless of whether
anyone can possibly seriously believe that I'm guilty."

"I know. We're working on it, Mayor."

"Well, what's the latest?"

"Nothing significant. I've got technicians checking the metal
detectors at the main entrance and in the lower rear entrance near
the chapel."

"They haven't found any problems with them?"

"Not yet. Listen, mind if I ask you a few questions?"

I sighed. That explained it. "Is that why you're here this morning?"

He didn't respond to that, just asked abruptly, "Why did you
hate Karl Krieg?"

"I didn't hate Karl Krieg. Come on, Charley, why are you questioning me again?"

"I'm the senior detective on the case."

"Since when?"

"The chief of detectives decided that since I was present at the
scene of the crime, I should head the team that breaks the case.
Your other regular bodyguards are on the team, too, since they
were also there that night. Now, would you answer the question,
please, Mayor?"

As mayor, I could not refuse to cooperate with the duly designated authorities. Besides, a lack of cooperation could be miscon-
strued by the opposition papers as an attempted cover-up of a
capital crime committed by one of my friends, or one of my commissioners.

"I didn't *hate* Karl Krieg. He once completed a job for the city
that was badly done and gave us a load of trouble, not to mention
the huge cost overruns. In my opinion, it would be harmful to the
city if he was ever given the opportunity to do another job for the
city."

"But only a few days ago, Mayor, at that press conference, you
said that," he consulted his notebook, "if Mr. Krieg applies for

sponsorship of the Muni Yard Project, he will be treated as well as any other applicant."

"And I meant it. Regardless of my feelings or experience with Krieg, if he entered the competition for the Muni Yard Project, he would be given a fair shake."

"Does that go for Commissioner Moshe Gur, too?"

"Absolutely. All members of my administration will apply all laws and regulations equally and equitably."

"Even though Commissioner Gur was known to have hated the victim?"

"Moshe Gur could no more treat anyone unfairly than he could use a chain saw on the Sabbath, regardless of his personal feelings."

"How about personal friends of yours, such as Mrs. Beverly Benson and Mr. Kenneth Lang?"

"How about them?"

"How well do you know them?"

"I know Mrs. Benson very well, and have for about eight years. Mr. Lang, I met only once before the wedding on Sunday. Still, I think they're both incapable of committing any crime worse than double parking."

Charley shrugged.

I looked out the window. We were crawling along busy Lexington Avenue now, passing the side entrances to Grand Central Station on the right. The sidewalks around the grand old stone building were jammed with people rushing to make trains or to get to work. Most of them had newspapers tucked under their arms—newspapers, I knew, that were filled with ridiculous implications about my involvement in the Krieg murder case.

I turned back to Charley, who promptly said, "Let me ask you something else."

"You might as well. In this traffic, we're going to be here awhile."

"Frank and Joan Mardin were not only Krieg's competitors, but had often stated publicly that he was a cheat, a crook, did shoddy work, and stole money from his jobs. Could they have killed him? One or the other, or both?"

"I know the firm slightly and, based on one experience, I have only good things to say about it. I met Mr. and Mrs. Mardin at the wedding—she did most of the talking while he listened. I got a favorable impression of her, and he seemed to be the strong silent type."

"How about Mrs. Krieg? She was the one in the red dress."

"No kidding, Charley. Who could miss her? Anyway, I don't know her personally, though she's been present at quite a few social affairs I've attended. But she seems to be nice enough, according to what I've heard."

"Why do you suppose a 'nice' woman married a man like Karl Krieg?"

"Why do *you* suppose?" I returned sarcastically. "Could it be for his money?"

"I'm asking you."

"How would I know?"

Charley glanced at his notes. "Several people witnessed Donna Krieg cozying up to Moshe Gur at the wedding reception. Why would she do that?"

"Maybe because she's a nice woman who was being used and manipulated by her husband to try to influence his getting the Muni Yard job. And I'm sure you didn't hear anything about Moshe Gur cozying up to her in return, because he would never do that."

He nodded. "Thank you for your help, Mayor. If you see or hear anything more—or remember anything—call me right away."

I agreed, and we rode in silence the rest of the way to City Hall.

As soon as I got upstairs, I stopped at Rosemary Larkin's desk and asked her to come into my office for a few minutes.

After she had shut the door behind her, I handed over the envelope.

"Thanks," she said. "Did this help?"

"You bet it did. I need a little more information," I said, "but it doesn't have to be in writing. Will you help me?"

Rosemary nodded. "I'll try. What do you want to know?"

"I'm sure the City Hall security police checked out the whole lower level the day before—maybe even the morning before—the Benson wedding. If they did, did they give the two bathrooms opposite the chapel a complete going-over? That is, not just the floor and the stalls, but did they look inside the tanks, underneath the sinks, in the toilet paper holders, places where somebody could've planted the murder weapon a day in advance so he could pick it up during the wedding?"

"I can tell you right now, because I'm preparing the bill for Mrs. Benson for the security part of the wedding. There was a complete shakedown of that whole area the morning of the wedding. Our security police are good; they're not only alert for daggers and guns, but for plastic explosives, drugs, and stuff like that. And toilet paper holders are too small to hold a dagger the size of the one that killed Krieg."

"That leads us to the next question," I said. "The guard at the station opposite the chapel door. Can you find out if her TV camera transmits everything it sees to the first floor central security bank to be recorded?"

"I already know that, too. All the interior cameras show their displays on the first floor monitor bank as well, and everything is recorded there."

"So there's a record of who on the staff used which bathroom before the—"

"Stop right there, Boss. If I were a suspicious type, I might think you were about to suggest that possibly one of our staff was paid what would be a huge amount of money for a civil servant to plant the dagger in a bathroom where the killer could find it an hour later."

"It's possible, Rosemary, and you know it."

She paused, then nodded reluctantly.

"See what you can find out. That's all I ask."

"All right . . ."

"Except, I need one more favor. I need to find the photographer for the Benson wedding. His name was Don O'Sullivan, if I remember correctly." Which I usually do, when it comes to names.

"You want me to get his number for you?" Rosemary asked, jotting the name on her ever-present pad.

"Please." I checked my watch. "Now, what do I have going on this morning?"

She handed over my agenda.

First up was a meeting with my press secretary, Jahn Ping, about the upcoming presentation of my twice-yearly Mayor's Management Report, which is the city's statistical report card.

After that, Moshe Gur was coming over to discuss how we were going to handle Krieg's death in terms of awarding the Muni Yard Project. I hadn't really spoken to Moshe, except to set up the meeting, since Sunday night, and I was anxious to hear what he had to say.

I scanned the rest of the list and looked at Rosemary. "Is Jahn here yet?"

"I'll go check on her."

"Thanks. And Rosemary, would you do me one last favor? Call the wedding caterer—Fab Affairs is the name. I'd like to see the woman who was in charge of the Benson-Lang wedding, today, late morning if possible, in my office. We can squeeze her in between my meeting with the cardinal and that awards luncheon at the Sherry Netherland."

"What do I tell her it's about?" Rosemary asked nervously. "You don't want her to think that she's a murder suspect."

"Of course I don't, if she doesn't think that already. I'm sure the detectives have already put her through the wringer. I just have to ask her a few questions."

Moshe Gur arrived precisely at ten. "Sorry I'm late," was the first thing he said. "Traffic is in gridlock because of that foreign diplomat, Mohammed what's his name, who's at the UN today."

"You're not late, Moshe," I said, pointing at the clock on the mantel of the fireplace to the left of my desk. "In fact, it's refreshing not to have you show up two hours early for a change."

He ignored my comment and opened his briefcase. "You wanted an update on the Muni Yard Project?"

"Yes, since I've got a press conference later to present my management report. They're bound to ask me about the Krieg thing."

"Do you want me to take the conference?"

"I'd love that, but they want to string me up, not you. I'll need you around, of course, and Jahn Ping, too, but I better have the

overall picture. For instance, what's been changed by Karl Krieg's murder?"

"As far as I'm concerned, personally and professionally, the situation has been greatly improved. Krieg was surely going to be the high bidder for the land; he didn't care how much of his investors' money he spent, as long as he got the job and could start draining money from the project. With him in the running, it was fairly certain that all the other bidders would go as high as possible— maybe as much as five or even ten percent above what they'd normally bid—in the hope that Krieg would be disqualified."

"Exactly," I said with a nod. "And now that Krieg isn't around . . ."

"We're not going to get as high bids from the rest of the interested developers," Moshe told me. "On the other hand, we'll save money. I guarantee—would have guaranteed—that with Krieg, the change orders and extras would start falling around our heads like autumn leaves before a shovel went into the ground, not to mention additional inspection and supervision, fighting about unwarranted claims, compliance with the contract, and following regulations and requirements."

"But there's no way to explain this to reporters, Moshe, particularly those who think in six-second sound bites. Did you see this morning's papers? There are already some editorials questioning the wisdom of going ahead with the project now that the greatest developer in the world is no longer around."

"I can't work in the way reporters want," Gur said. "I can only do and say what is professionally and financially sound. You know my record, Mayor. I'm a good technician and administrator and a bad public relations commissioner. I have a good PR woman but, frankly, there's only one person who can talk to the press about this in the way it should be presented, and that's you. I'll back you up with technical and financial information."

"Thanks. Now, listen, Moshe, I have another problem I have to talk to you about."

"It's about Krieg, too, isn't it?"

I nodded. "This thing reflects on the whole administration, so I have to gather all the facts I can."

"The police—Charley Deacon—have already interviewed me, Mayor. Ruth, too."

"Ruth?"

"Yes, and she was very upset afterward. Ever since her mother died in February, she's been emotionally fragile. And now she's worried that the police think we had something to do with Krieg's death. But, as I told her, it's Charley's job to speak with everybody who was there and to suspect everybody who was there. And the worst part is, all the most likely suspects are your friends or acquaintances."

I shook my head. "Not just my friends—me too."

"I know," Moshe said. "I've seen the papers."

"I have to figure out who the real killer is, Moshe. That's why I have to ask you some questions, and please don't read anything into this."

"But you don't think that I—"

"I don't think anything. Listen, it's clear that Krieg was killed between the time that all the stacks of chairs were taken out of the alcoves and the time I walked to the front where the lectern was. Where were you during that period?"

"Somewhere along the back wall, on the right side of the aisle as I faced front, near the middle. There was a narrow space—like an aisle—about three feet wide between the last row of chairs and the wall, and I was near the chairs, looking for Ruth so that we could sit together."

"Did you see anyone you knew in that area? Or near it?"

"Mr. Lang, Mr. Mardin, Mr. and Mrs. Benson. You, of course. Mrs. Krieg—she kept trying to talk to me, not that I gave her the time of day—and one of Deacon's men."

"You had to have seen more people than that."

"At least five or six, but I didn't know them."

"Did you hear any unusual sounds?"

"What, you mean like groans, or Krieg's fat body hitting the floor?" Moshe asked wryly. "It was pretty noisy, what with the stacks of chairs being brought out and taken apart."

"Did you see Karl Krieg?"

"At the beginning, when they started taking out the chairs, I saw him on the side, near the back, to my right. Just for a moment.

I got the impression he was trying to get to the back aisle, but I was looking for Ruth, not him."

I nodded. "Thanks, Moshe. If there's anything else you remember, no matter how trivial, let me know at once." I hesitated, but I had to say it. "I don't think it'll be necessary, but if I have to talk to Ruth . . . ?"

Moshe thought for a moment. "If it's absolutely necessary . . ."

"I'll do my best to make it unnecessary," I promised, checking my watch. "I've got a meeting with the cardinal in about two minutes, so . . ."

"Okay, I'm going," he said, getting up. "See you at the press conference. And good luck."

"You know me," I said. "Once I start talking, I'll be brilliant."

The caterer, Hinda Grisin, looked a lot less imposing in a business suit and high heels than she had when she wore the white tuxedo and the red carnation.

"Thank you for coming on such short notice," I said, shaking her hand as she entered my office.

"It's okay," she told me. "We have very few affairs to cater at this time on a weekday."

After she was seated, I said, "I'd like to speak to you about something."

"Can I assume you aren't interested in hiring Fab Affairs to cater a party, Mr. Mayor?"

"You can, although I was very impressed by the efficiency of your operation."

"Our people are trained professionals. We pay them more than any other caterers I know, we charge our clients more, and we do better. If the city has any need for catering—no job too large, no job too small—try us, you'll be pleased."

"I usually don't make those decisions, but I'll be glad to mention your name to those who do."

"Thank you." She paused only a moment before saying, "You asked me here to talk about the murder."

"Well, yes." I liked her straightforward manner.

She got up. "That's what I thought. Neither I nor my associates had anything to do with the murder or know anything about it."

"Please sit down. I don't doubt that, but there are things you know about that could help us."

She sat down. "Ask."

"Is there any possibility that the dagger—the murder weapon—was brought in with the food and drink?"

"Impossible. I examine every container for damage before it's opened. If it's cracked, I treat it as contaminated. I'm present at the opening of every container and the removal of every bit of the food and its placement on the serving trays. This affair was only cold, dry appetizers, previously prepared, in bite-size pieces."

"How about the beer and ice barrels? Could someone have . . . ?"

"Same thing. I'm there to open and to taste. If there was a knife at the bottom of the ice barrel, the bartender would have to act very funny—reach his whole arm in to get it and get his jacket sleeve wet—and I would notice or the other bartender would notice."

"I suppose you would," I agreed, thinking that she appeared to have graduated from the Rosemary Larkin school of no-nonsense, sharp-eyed observation.

"Believe me, Mr. Mayor, none of my people is crazy enough to smuggle in a weapon. Besides, what about the metal detector?"

"Under the right conditions," I said, "a metal detector can be bypassed. The one at the rear entrance, for example. We had only one security officer at the metal detector there and one near the chapel. The one outside the chapel had to divide her attention among the chapel door, the two bathrooms, and the stairway from the first floor, and the whole basement corridor."

"So what's your point?"

"Just this: If one of your people were to throw the wrapped knife over the detector to another of your people at the exact moment that neither the detector officer or the area officer was looking that way, the knife could get past the detector. The inside man would then slip the knife into his pocket and go into the chapel."

"So, you're saying," Hinda Grisin told me, "that if two officers are not paying attention at the same time that two of my people, one on each side of the detector, are playing games and, also at the same time, none of my other people are looking on, it might work."

"Exactly." I had to admit, the theory didn't make much sense, but I had to stay with it. "And one minute later, the knife is in the killer's hands."

"How?"

"The waiter takes it out of his pocket and hands it to the killer with a canape?"

"Where a hundred people can see it? Or hear it drop when the killer fumbles the transfer?"

"The killer meets the waiter in the men's room, maybe?"

"I'm sorry, Mr. Mayor," Grisin said, "but this idea depends on too many coincidences and on everything working perfectly."

I knew she was right about that, and admitted it. "But what if there was no exchange between the waiter and the killer? What if the waiter *was* the killer?"

"Impossible."

"Nothing's impossible."

"Let me explain something about our business. I'm one of the owners, so this is fact. We don't know until the day of the affair who is going to work. People get sick, transportation breaks down, an emergency arises, a hundred reasons. Whoever's in charge—me, in this case—decides who goes with her to work the job."

"So you're saying there's no way the killer, if it were one of your people, would be guaranteed they'd be working at the chapel that day."

"Not only that, but I run such a tight ship that there's no way any of my people could smuggle anything in. The kitchen people prepare the food and drink, the servers put on the appropriate clothes from the clothing storage room, everybody goes to the toilet, everybody washes up, I inspect, and then we go. The pockets of the clothes are sewn closed. This makes for a better fit and nobody has a handkerchief. Guests don't want to see servers using handkerchiefs."

"No, I don't suppose they do."

Hinda Grisin was on a roll. "None of my people goes into any bathroom the guests use; the last thing I need is a guest seeing one of my people in a bathroom. Even worse, is one of my staff washing his hands. Absolute catastrophe is seeing one of us *not* washing his hands—not that it happens, you understand. But *if* it ever did, one guest would tell another and that minute, I'm out of business."

"I can imagine," I murmured, nodding.

"So, Mr. Mayor, that knife did not come from us, through us, or by us. I'm sorry to say this, but one of Mrs. Benson's guests did it. Maybe even one of her own friends, at her daughter's wedding. It's a shame, but it has to be true."

She got up. "I don't think there's any more I can tell you. You want to see how we work, come to our shop."

"I don't think," I said, "that anything I see at your shop will be half as impressive as you are, Mrs. Grisin. I'm convinced."

"Good. Catch the killer," she said firmly. "Dead bodies at my affairs are even worse than a staff member not washing his hands."

NINE

It wasn't until later that afternoon that I finally had the chance to dial the number Rosemary had given me for Don O'Sullivan's photography studio. It had a 718 area code, which meant either Brooklyn or Queens.

"Don O'Sullivan," he answered cheerfully on the second ring.

"Mr. O'Sullivan, this is Ed Koch."

"Oh, yeah, right. Come on, Johnny, I'm not falling for it this time."

I frowned. "Mr. O'Sullivan?"

There was a moment of silence.

Then he said, "Oh, God, this really is you, isn't it, Mr. Mayor?"

"Yup. Who's Johnny?"

"A friend of mine. Just a few weeks ago, he called and told me he was with one of the big modeling agencies and wanted me for a shoot. He had me going until I realized it was April Fools' Day."

"Well, today isn't April Fools' Day, and this really is Ed Koch, and I have to be at a press conference in about two minutes, so I'm going to make this fast."

"Sure, I'm listening."

"Have you developed the film from the Benson wedding yet?"

"I did it first thing Monday. A Sergeant Deacon from the NYPD asked for prints."

"So he already has them?"

"Yeah, and I don't think the bride and groom are going to be very happy about that, since they haven't even seen them yet. But they're in Hawaii, and besides, when the police ask you to do something—"

"And when the mayor asks you to do something," I cut in, "you do it. Right?"

He hesitated only briefly. "Right."

"So, Don, you won't mind making a set of prints for me then, will you? At my expense, of course."

"I . . . I guess it would be okay. When do you—"

"Tomorrow," I said firmly. "I'll come by to pick them up in person. I want to ask you a few questions, too."

"You too? Sergeant Deacon already put me through the third degree. Listen, you don't think that I—"

"Of course I don't. I just want to see if you noticed anything unusual while you were making the rounds at the wedding ceremony and reception."

"I didn't."

"We'll see," I said. "Now, where is your studio, and when is a good time?"

"Any time—I'll be here all day. And I'm in Queens, in Long Island City. It's actually my home, too. On Forty-seventh Avenue."

"Fine. I'm going to transfer you to my secretary so that you can give her the exact address and directions. She'll set up an appointment based on my schedule. Okay?"

"Okay."

"Thanks, Mr. O'Sullivan."

"You're welcome, Mr. Mayor."

Feeling a great sense of accomplishment, I transferred him over to Rosemary, then gathered up my notes.

The press conference was held in the City Hall Press Room. I walked over with Jahn Ping, so that we could go over, once again, the statement I had prepared about the Muni Yard Project.

Jahn's skin is like fine porcelain and she is so small and slim she looks like she'd break if handled even slightly roughly. But her sharp tongue could slice a grown man into coleslaw if he irritated her, and do it before the smug fool even knew he was being zapped.

Not that Jahn was belligerent; a courteous question got a polite answer, an intelligent question—as opposed to one whose only function was to make the Administration look foolish or ignorant—got a responsive, carefully thought-out answer.

Jahn never lied, but she was a genius at giving accurate, verifiable answers that sounded complete but didn't quite emphasize any mistake I'd made. She had to be. While I knew that the only way not to make a mistake is not to stick your neck out, that's not my style.

"Now, when they ask you about the murder itself, remember my rule of thumb."

"And which one is that?"

Jahn smiled. "The one about how when we have nothing to say, we make things dull, dull, dull, with a little uninteresting thrown in, along with a touch of boring. They want excitement and intrigue, let them use their imaginations."

"They already have been, according to the papers," I said dryly. "Some of the tabloids have made me out to be the most interesting criminal to hit this town since that kissing bandit was stalking women in that health club last summer."

We went into the Press Room, where Moshe was waiting, along with the usual crowd of reporters. I placed my notes on the lectern and, without much ado, began reading the statement about the Rail Yard.

Basically, I told them that Karl Krieg had been murdered, that the situation would have no impact on the bidding for the Rail Yard, and that it would be business as usual as the city evaluated the project and reached a conclusion regarding its development.

There were a few questions about the project itself, and I managed to field them nicely, without Moshe's intervention.

Then a reporter near the back asked, "What do you have to say about the murder itself, Mr. Mayor?"

"Just this: If you want information, you'll have to check with the police."

"Is it true you're a suspect?"

"In the sense that anybody in the chapel at the time of the

homicide might be a suspect, I guess I could be considered one . . . but again, you have to ask the police."

"Is it true, Mr. Mayor, that everybody in that chapel was a supporter of yours?"

"That's ridiculous! I don't know who my supporters are. I know that I vote for myself. Beyond that, it's anyone's guess who people support."

"Mr. Mayor, are you willing to cooperate with the investigation if it turns out that one of your friends is a prime suspect?"

"I'm *always* willing to cooperate with a police investigation."

I picked up my notes. Then I said abruptly, and, I might add, truthfully, "I'm hungry. This press conference is over."

When I got to Lolly's apartment, she and Beverly Benson were on the couch, looking thoroughly relaxed. Bevvy even looked happy to see me.

"Ed! You look wonderful. How have you been?" she asked, as though we hadn't seen each other in ages.

"Hungry. You know what encounters with the press do to my appetite," I said, mostly to Lolly, who obliged by handing me a basket of crackers that had been sitting on the coffee table.

I took a couple and said, "Well? Are we going to get this over with so that we can go to dinner?"

"I have a tape machine in my office next door," Lolly said, standing up. "Follow me."

There was a door at the end of the foyer that she opened with a key. She led us into her spacious home office, which I had only seen once or twice before. It's bright and cheery, with framed modern art prints on the whitewashed walls, and curtained windows that display a perfect view of the river.

Bevvy handed her the tape cassette.

Lolly slipped it into an expensive-looking machine and looked at me. "Ready?"

"Wait a minute. First, Bevvy, when was this call made?"

"Last Friday, 10:00 A.M. We keep track of all calls in a bound log, not a loose-leaf—full details, when, who, why, result, and action to be taken. But all that's unimportant now; I'm just showing you why you shouldn't even consider suspecting me."

"And I'm just trying to cover all the bases."

"So why don't you cover the base Lolly's on?" Bevvy asked shrewdly.

"Because I'm a witness that she didn't do it."

"And there's no way she can outsmart you? Fool you?"

"It isn't a question of outsmarting or fooling; I was watching her."

"During the time the murder took place, right? And you know for sure when the murder took place? It couldn't have been two minutes earlier or two minutes later?"

"I'm almost positive."

"Almost. But you could easily be two minutes off, and even three or four, earlier or later. Maybe even five or six." She looked satisfied.

"Look, let's just listen to the tape," I said. "I'm anxious to hear what happened between you and Karl."

Lolly pressed Play, and after a few seconds of dead air, it began.

BEVVY: This is Beverly Benson in person, not my secretary, the one who's called you three times this morning. I want to speak with Mr. Krieg *now*. I know he's in so don't give me that bull about his being out. Tell Mr. Krieg that the reason I sound angry is because I am angry. It's very, *very* important that I speak to him because if I don't, I'm not going to call him again and when he calls me, as he will, I'm going to be out to him permanently.

SECRETARY: Hold on, please.

(CLICK, DEAD AIR, ANOTHER CLICK)

KRIEG: Hello, Beverly; nice to hear from you.

BEVVY: It would be nice to hear from you too, Karl. My third payment is almost thirty days overdue.

KRIEG: A minor oversight, Beverly. I'll take care of it shortly.

BEVVY: I'm used to dealing in real numbers, Karl; how many hours is shortly?

KRIEG: I'm a little too busy right now to be pinned down, Bev, honey.

BEVVY: Like you were a little too busy last month and the month before, Karl, darling?

KRIEG: Relax, Beverly; doesn't your contract call for interest at two points over prime on any late payments?

BEVVY: For a maximum of fifteen days late; you're almost ninety days past due.

KRIEG: So all I'm doing is paying you more than you expected.

BEVVY: No, Karl; you're paying me a lot less than I expected. Like nothing. Zero. I turned down solid, dependable accounts because you caught me first, and then my people worked like dogs to get the papers and applications and everything ready for when you wanted them. On top of that, it was my reputation that got you a hearing at all. And the icing on the cake is, I have a damn good idea who leaked to the press that you, with the help of Beverly Benson, had sewn up the deal for the Muni Yard, which forced Koch to say that you would be treated equally with the other applicants. And now you're telling me I'm not getting paid at all?

KRIEG: I never said you wouldn't get paid. As soon as I—

BEVVY: Not "as soon as." Now. All of it. In one hour I'm sending you a registered letter saying that according to the contract you owe me a million nine in fees alone, plus the expenses I've laid out, plus the contractual interest. So if this is the only language you understand, listen carefully. Right after you get that letter, my attorney will sue you for business lost due to your actions and he'll subpoena all the papers I've made out to see how you've changed them to make you look better. And just for good luck, my attorney will prepare a lien against the property and let it be known to all the bonding companies and insurance companies that it's ready to be served in case you should con the city into awarding you anything. Your performance and payment bonds will be pulled so fast that—

KRIEG: Nobody talks to me that way, Benson. I was going to send you something, but if that's your attitude, go ahead and sue. It's your money that's tied up, not mine.

BEVVY: Some people think that because I'm a woman, I can be pushed around. I *can't* be pushed around and I *won't* be pushed around. So let's talk sense. It's not my money that's tied up, it's your life. You think, when I fill out a professional and business history of a client and his companies, that I take his word for everything, that I don't investigate? My people are careful and accurate, and they know how to get information. And when my first bill isn't paid in time, I take certain precautions.

KRIEG: What the hell are you talking about?

BEVVY: On the strength of what the mayor said, you're hoping to get some big money from investors in Singapore. You intend to use that money to pay off people like me and to drain off some of that money for your personal needs. There's only one problem. These people are at least as smart as you are, and they'll examine the papers I prepared very carefully. When they do, they may find some things that will make them take the first plane home without even saying good-bye to you. They may even find out these things from other sources; papers have a tendency to leak, as you know.

KRIEG: What the hell did you do?

BEVVY: I just discovered that the papers we've been sending you the past two months were actually work sheets, not really complete or accurate. Of course, we'll have the final papers ready shortly.

KRIEG: I'll have my people, my accountants, go over—

BEVVY: You think those cheap amateurs will do in three weeks what took us three months to complete? As for the minimum-wage jerks working for you, maybe some of them can read, but understanding technical and legal jargon is not really their strong suit. My husband, as you know, is a bond broker who's used to reading very fine print, and when I gave him a few papers to check, he couldn't find even one of the little problems that were buried in there. (PAUSE) I'm so glad we had this little talk. Good-bye, dahling.

KRIEG: Wait. I'll pay a third.

BEVVY: All.

KRIEG: Two-thirds; that's all I can raise fast.

BEVVY: That shows you're really not qualified to enter the game.

KRIEG: All right, all. I'll send you a check tomorrow.

BEVVY: That'll be fine. As soon as the check clears—and I mean the bank it's written on, even if it's in the Cayman Islands—and the deposit is solidly in my bank account for three full working days, I'll send you the papers. I'll also want a complete disclaimer, a release, a hold harmless, and anything else my lawyer insists on.

KRIEG: I can't wait that long; I'll bring you a check on a local bank.

BEVVY: A major local bank, and have your attorney write the papers that protect me and fax them to my lawyer along with a check for his fees and costs.

KRIEG: I don't have time; make it your attorney who—

BEVVY: My attorney is very slow and very expensive. Isn't there one lawyer in New York who trusts you?

KRIEG: Okay, cash.

BEVVY: In my bank's office. This is the money you've been hiding from your wife, right?

KRIEG: The bank's open Sunday?

BEVVY: You know damn well it isn't.

KRIEG: That's how long it'll take me to get it.

BEVVY: Monday morning; my daughter's getting married Sunday.

KRIEG: I know; I got the invite.

BEVVY: And you just got the disinvite.

KRIEG: My wife is really looking forward to it. And I need the papers for Monday morning.

BEVVY: No way am I going to take two million from you—anything from you—at Aileen's wedding.

KRIEG: I'll turn it into a check as soon as the banks open Monday morning. Make sure that my papers—the good ones—are ready.

BEVVY: A certified check on a major local bank, along with a waiver of any right to recall the certification.

KRIEG: You got a suspicious mind, Benson.

BEVVY: Comes from making mistakes in picking clients, and don't change the subject. If my lawyer accepts the releases, I'll phone you to tell you which bank. And stay away from the wedding.

KRIEG: I still need you around to keep my investors happy. What're you gonna do if I show up? Throw me and Donna out? You be nice and I'll be nice. A deal's a deal.

BEVVY: I won't throw you out personally, Krieg; I'll just have you barred by the security cops.

KRIEG: If that's what you really want; no hard feelings. Donna bought a nice present for Aileen and I'll be bringing the one you asked me for when we first got together. Fifty grand in cash. On the envelope it'll say, 'For BB, as agreed.' I'll leave the envelope unsealed, so in case I drop it and some bills fall out, the cop at the metal detector who bars me will know what to do.

BEVVY: I never paid off anybody in my life, you lying bastard.

KRIEG: See you at the wedding. (PHONE HUNG UP)

Reaching over and pushing the Stop button on the tape player, Bevvy looked at me triumphantly. "Okay, now, Ed?" she said. "I'm off the list of suspects?"

I really liked Bevvy most of the time, so I chose my words carefully. "If I were you, and I'm speaking not just as a friend, but as a lawyer—though not as your lawyer, of course—I wouldn't let anyone listen to that tape. And I'm sorry I heard it."

"What the hell are you talking about?" Bevvy asked shrilly, as Lolly looked at me in amazement.

"Calm down, Bevvy," I said.

"Why should I kill a guy, even if he's a creep and a crooked bastard, who's going to give me two million plus the next morning?

I mean, even if I wanted to kill him for real, even if I *intended* to kill him for real, couldn't I have waited till the next morning, after I collected what he owed me, to do it?"

"That's perfectly logical, but logic doesn't always come into play in a court," I said. "Let me show you what it could be like."

"Oh, please do," Bevvy said bitterly, waving a slender hand. "Show me how anyone could possibly incriminate me, based on *nothing.*"

"The prosecutor tells the jury that he will show that you hated the deceased—just listen to how you sound on the tape—and that you were ready, able, and willing to destroy Krieg financially. Not only to put him out of business, but to cause him to lose his whole business which, at his age, he'd never be able to recover."

"But—"

"I'm not finished. Through deliberately putting mistakes and inconsistencies in the work you were doing for him profession-ally—which shows your lack of integrity—you were not only going to pauperize him, but you were going to ruin his reputation so that he would not only lose the biggest project of his life, but you were going to arrange it so he could never even borrow money from overseas. And think of what it would sound like when he tells the jury that you were summoned to testify before a Grand Jury, not once, but twice."

"I was cleared each time. It was because of two incompetent employees that I fired."

"And you even threatened to kill him."

"Never!"

"On the tape you said that it was his life that was tied up. How do you think a clever prosecutor would interpret that?"

"It wasn't meant that way; it was . . ." Bevvy paused and pressed her fingertips to her temples, closing her eyes. "Krieg was a liar and a thief who was trying to steal my work and using my reputation to get the biggest project of his life and to finance every-thing by getting investors from Singapore to foot the whole bill without putting in a penny of his own."

"All that may be true," I said, more gently, "but it will certainly be very hard to prove, if not impossible. More importantly, it strengthens your motive to kill him."

Her eyes snapped open again and she looked sharply at me. "You haven't said anything about why I'd possibly kill Krieg before I collected whatever he owed me."

"Did he call you again?"

"Certainly not, and my logs will show it."

"Suppose he called you at home from a pay phone. Do you log your home phone calls?"

"No, that's personal."

"And he told you that even though he delivered the harmless papers, he'd decided not to pay you. So that adds to your motive and now there's no longer any reason to wait till Monday to kill him. Go prove the two of you didn't speak again. You weren't exactly friendly to him at the chapel."

"So I made the knife in two days and hid it in my bra?"

"You had the knife made—any kid could do it—and as mother of the bride, you could have been all over the chapel long before the wedding. Everybody here and in the Municipal Building knows you and wouldn't stop you."

"I swear he didn't call. I had every expectation that he'd pay me Monday."

"Even if he didn't call, I saw Krieg come into the chapel with his wife, and though you didn't shake his hand, he said a few words to you. Could those words have been that he had decided not to pay you the next day, since he'd already arranged another source of money? And since now that he was being seen in a small gathering with the mayor, he didn't need you anymore?"

"All he said was that he'd see me tomorrow morning."

"Do you have any way to prove that? Do you have any more tapes of his calls?"

"I told you, he didn't call again and as far as I know, no one overheard what he said to me when he came into the chapel." Bevvy was not looking as happy as she had when she started playing the tape. "How do you prove you didn't do something?" She was close to tears.

"Exactly. You can't prove your innocence; all you can do is prove someone else guilty. Which is what I'm trying to do. For that, I need your help, Bevvy."

"That's enough, Ed," Lolly said heavily. "Leave her alone."

"Okay, then I'll talk with you. At the reception in the chapel, Bevvy came to you and asked you to do something for the good of the wedding. To go over to Ken Lang and entertain him all the time until the ceremony started. She started giving you phony reasons, and when you objected, she pulled you aside and told you the real reason. When you went over to Ken, Bevvy told me the deal was that I had to check in with you every five minutes, which I couldn't do because I kept getting waylaid. Anyway, you left Ken a couple of minutes before the ceremony started."

"So what's the problem?" Lolly asked. "How much could he drink in those few minutes? I wanted to get a front seat."

"You told me that Ken Lang recently swore he'd kill Karl Krieg."

"I also said that half the people in New York have sworn the same thing."

"Ken didn't do it," Bevvy said. "He's a very sweet, gentle man. I've known him for over a year and if there's one thing I know, it's men."

"Do you want to be present when I question him?" I asked.

"God, no; he's my in-law. If he even thinks I'm involved in something like that . . . I don't want Aileen and Alan to . . . Do you have to, Ed?"

"I'm afraid I do, Bevvy."

She sighed. "That man isn't just my friend, he's part of my family now. What if you find out something that—"

"That's the whole point," I interrupted. "For God's sake, Bevvy, the only way I'm going to clear my name, and yours, too, for that matter, is to find the real killer. And if Ken Lang's the one, then that's his problem."

"If Ken Lang's the one, I'll be totally shocked."

Frankly, so would I.

But then, someone at that wedding had killed Karl Krieg— someone that I knew personally. And if I didn't figure out who it was, I might as well kiss City Hall and Gracie Mansion good-bye.

_____ TEN

"Mr. Mayor . . ."
"Mr. Mayor . . ."
"Mr. Mayor . . ."

I sighed and turned to face the throng of reporters on the steps of City Hall Wednesday morning.

"Mr. Mayor, the murder was committed on Sunday afternoon," one of them, an attractive blonde from a local news station, said, "right under the noses of a hundred important people, including you. It's already Wednesday and there have been no arrests. What do you think about that?"

"What do I think about that? I think that our police department is conducting a thorough investigation, and that when they have sufficient evidence to make an arrest, they will."

"But why is it taking so long?" someone called from the outskirts of the throng.

"I just said that the police department is conducting a _thorough_ investigation, and that obviously takes time."

"How could a crime of this magnitude take place right in City Hall? What does that say about security and the police officers who were there when Karl Krieg was murdered?"

"Did any of you genuises take a look at my management report, which was released yesterday? If you had, you would have noticed that over the first four months of the current fiscal year, the overall crime rate dropped significantly, and the total number of arrests rose considerably. I'd say that record speaks for itself."

The diversion to my report changed the course of questioning, just as I had intended it to. For the next few minutes, I answered queries about the number of watermain breaks and the percentage of restaurants that had passed inspection and so on.

Finally, I called it quits and headed inside, with Marv and the other bodyguards surrounding me, as usual.

I checked my schedule with Rosemary. The meeting with Don O'Sullivan was set for later this morning, sandwiched between my eight o'clock meeting with two of my deputy mayors, and a ribbon-cutting ceremony in Astoria, Queens, which was certainly convenient, since Astoria is adjacent to Long Island City.

Even more convenient: As I had hoped, today was one of the rare days when I didn't already have a lunch meeting scheduled. Perfect.

As soon as I was settled in my leather chair in my office, a cup of steaming black coffee in my hand, I called Ken Lang at his office. The machine picked up on the second ring, so I left a message asking him to call me back as soon as possible.

Next, I dialed 4-1-1.

When Information answered, I asked for the number of Jomar Development Corporation in Brooklyn.

"What is the name of the firm, sir?"

"Jomar. J-O-M-A-R," I said, and tapped my pen impatiently against the legal pad in my lap.

I swiftly jotted the number she gave, then dialed it and hoped that Frank and Joan weren't nine-to-fivers. It wasn't even eight o'clock yet, but with any luck . . .

"Jomar Development."

If I wasn't mistaken, that was Joan Mardin's voice answering the phone. But just in case, I said, "Are either Joan or Frank in, please?"

"Who may I say is calling?"

"Mayor Koch."

The slightest pause, and then, "Mayor Koch—it's me, Joan. I always get in early so that I can get things done before actual business hours, when the phone starts ringing off the hook."

"Then I'll make this quick—"

"Oh, I didn't mean it like that. I meant—"

"I know, it's okay. Listen, are you free for lunch today?"

There was a long moment of silence.

I suddenly realized that she was wondering what to make of the question, and quickly added, "You *and* your husband, of course."

"Oh, of course," she said, sounding relieved. "I believe we are . . ."

"Then would you both like to join me at Le Café Jacques on East Fifty-fifth Street?"

I'd chosen that restaurant for two reasons. One, it was convenient to the Queensborough Bridge, so I could easily get there after that ribbon-cutting ceremony. And two, the chef, Hugo, does amazing things with grilled lamb, and my mouth was watering just thinking about it.

Joan agreed, of course, to the lunch date, and we settled on one o'clock, which would give me just enough time to get back from Astoria. After we hung up, I buzzed Rosemary and told her to make a reservation, and to send the deputy mayors, Darnell Watts and Sylvia Rosenthal, into my office.

It was time to put the murder on hold once again while I tended to my first responsibility and priority: running the city I loved.

Don O'Sullivan's Long Island City neighborhood isn't exactly the most upscale one in town, but I'm familiar enough with it to know that there are lots of great loft spaces for low rent . . . not to mention a couple of excellent diners where you can still get a full dinner, including an appetizer, coffee, and dessert, for around ten bucks.

My bodyguards didn't look thrilled when we pulled up in front of the shabby three-story building that bore the address Rosemary had written down.

Flanked by two of them, with another cautiously proceeding ahead, I arrived on the doorstep and rang the bell for apartment 3A. There was a prompt buzz and the door clicked to let me in.

The hallway smelled like frying onions and Lysol, and the stairs creaked as we climbed to the third floor.

Don O'Sullivan was waiting in the open doorway at the top

landing. "Mr. Mayor, come on in," he said, reaching out to shake my hand.

He escorted me into an open loft space that was surprisingly bright and sunny for such a dingy building. Two walls were exposed brick, the other two painted white, and the high ceilings and minimalist decor gave the place an airy feel.

"Have a seat," Don offered, gesturing at the futon in one corner. "Would you like some coffee?"

"Actually, I wish I could, but I've got to get to a ribbon-cutting ceremony in Astoria, so I'll make this quick."

"In that case," Don said, going over to a battered worktable under the window and picking up a bulging manila envelope, "I'll hand these over right now."

"Thanks," I said, taking it from him and peeking inside at the stacks of photos. I reached into my pocket and took out my checkbook. "What do I owe you?"

"It's okay, you don't have to—"

I insisted, and he finally named a figure. I promptly wrote out a check and handed it over.

"Now that that's settled," I said, "let me ask you a few fast questions. First, did you notice anything unusual at the ceremony?"

He shook his head. "Like I told you before, I really didn't. I was too busy concentrating on snapping pictures of the guests. Aileen and Alan had told me that they wanted lots of candid shots."

I nodded. "Can I ask how you were chosen as the photographer for the wedding?" I was thinking that I couldn't imagine Bevvy Benson using someone who wasn't one of the handful of "name" photographers in Manhattan.

As though he had read my mind, Don laughed ruefully and said, "You're right, big society weddings aren't my usual assignments. But Alan and I were fraternity brothers in college, and he convinced Aileen and her mother that I should photograph the wedding. And I did an excellent job, if I do say so myself," he added, a little defensively.

"I'm sure you did. As you were going around snapping candids, did you happen to see Karl Krieg?"

"I didn't pay too much attention to him, though he is in the background of some of the pictures I got. Couldn't miss his wife, though. I snapped her talking to that short, bearded guy who was some kind of nut, if you ask me."

He had to mean Moshe Gur. "What do you mean, he was some kind of nut?"

"He had this gorgeous blonde—who was bursting out of that red dress, in case you didn't notice—trying to hang all over him, and he looked like he was trying to escape the whole time."

Yup, it was Moshe Gur, all right. "Did you hear any of their conversation?"

"Nope. Like I said, I was too busy concentrating on taking pictures."

I questioned Don O'Sullivan for a few more minutes, but it was clear that he had nothing new to tell me.

I glanced at my watch and stood up, tucking the envelope under my arm. "I really appreciate your cooperation, Mr. O'Sullivan," I said sincerely.

"No problem. I hope you catch whoever did it, and if the pictures help, I'll be glad. But I've gone over them a bunch of times in the past few days, and I can't find anything unusual in them. Maybe you'll have better luck."

"You never know." I shook his hand, thanked him again, and, with my bodyguards bustling around me, headed back down to the limo, which looked distinctly out of place on the seedy street in front of the building.

I arrived at Le Café Jacques a few minutes early, thanks to lighter-than-usual traffic on the Queensborough Bridge. After the ribbon-cutting ceremony, I had even had time to stop in at my favorite Greek bakery on Ditmars Boulevard, where my old pal George Caviros had insisted on presenting me with some of his excellent baklava.

Now, as I made my way through the crowded dining room, a few people called out greetings.

"How'm I doin'?" I asked cheerfully in response, stopping here and there to chat and shake hands. Not one person brought up the murder or the fact that the papers were calling me a suspect, which just goes to show you the kind of crowd that frequents the place: tactful and polite.

The Mardins showed up right on time. Caught in the middle of the workday, they obviously hadn't been prepared for as posh a place as Le Café Jacques.

Joan was wearing low heels with a plain, practical blouse and skirt, and looked a lot shorter than when I had seen her at the wedding. Frank, her taller husband, was in a set of work denims, clean and pressed, but with a few oil stains and not really in keeping with the dignified luxury of the elegant dining room.

"I had hoped to get home to change, but I didn't get the chance," he explained after we'd been seated.

"In the future," his wife said, "we'll have to keep an extra set of clothes at the office."

To help put them at ease, I ordered gin and tonics all around, the large amount of tonic to help wet the dry throats—the Mardins had to know what they were here for—and the gin to relax any tensions.

I said it anyway, as soon as the waiter had discreetly filled our water glasses and taken our orders.

"I asked you here, Mr. and Mrs. Mardin, because, as an interested citizen, I'm looking into the killing of Karl Krieg. At about the time of the murder, both of you, along with me and several others, were in the back row of the chapel near where Krieg was killed. Please tell me what you saw."

"Nothing, really," Joan said, with a glance at her husband. "Nothing unusual, that is. Just a lot of people waiting for a chance to sit down and watch the ceremony. Which wasn't much, I must say. I mean, this was the first nonreligious ceremony I'd seen, and it was sort of—sort of bland—no offense to you, of course, Mr. Mayor."

"Of course. And please call me Ed."

"When Joan and I got married," Frank said, "we had a big Jewish ceremony with all the rituals that go along with that. It was special." He took his wife's hand and patted it affectionately.

"I agree with you," I said. "As mayor, I get invited to more weddings of all denominations than I could possibly attend, and every one of them is a better ritual than the civil ceremony. But

there are many people who aren't religious, so for them a civil ceremony in the Municipal Building serves its purpose."

Although the discussion of weddings was interesting, the purpose of this meeting was to question the suspects, and I didn't
want to get sidetracked.

I was about to jump back to my original topic when Frank excused himself to go to the men's room. After he had left the table,
walking with a slight limp and looking vaguely self-conscious
amidst the well-heeled lunch crowd, I turned to Joan.

"Who did you see," I asked her, "near you at the time the
chairs were being set up?"

"I saw Frank, of course, but I had to go ahead and hold two
chairs; he can't move as fast as I can on account of an old hip
injury. Then Karl Krieg, on the side over to my right, and Moshe
Gur, Donna Krieg—I saw her come in with Karl; you couldn't
miss her—Bevvy Benson, Mrs. Winter, whom I'd never seen
before that day, and some people I didn't know. Actually, I did see
Mr. Lang, but I didn't know who he was until the ceremony
began. He was talking with Mrs. Winter."

"But that was before all the chairs were set out."

She nodded. "When about half of the chairs were out, I was
busy looking for a pair of chairs near the aisle."

"You found the chairs?"

"I ran and got them, third row, right on the aisle."

"How long before your husband joined you?"

"A minute or two; there were a lot of people trying to get at the
good seats."

The waiter reappeared with a basket of what I knew were the
most delicate, flaky rolls I have ever encountered. As he was leaving, Frank returned.

We all helped ourselves to the rolls, and I continued with my
questioning. "Right after he came in, I noticed that Krieg came
over to both of you as soon as he saw you. Of all the people in the
chapel."

"The man had no tact," Joan said. "No dignity."

"I pulled away as soon as he came near," Frank said. "I didn't
want to leave Joan alone with the bastard, but if I'd stayed, I knew

I would've had to slug him and spoil the wedding for Bevvy Benson."

"So you left your wife alone with Krieg?"

"She's handled worse and she knows how to do it quietlike. She's half-owner of the company and what she decides, I go along with."

"Regardless of what it is?"

"We're married," Frank said, "and that's how we do it. It goes both ways. Usually we discuss important things, but if there's no time, one of us does what has to be done. I decide something, that's it. Joan decides something, that's it. Besides, she does all the talking."

"I was watching," I said to Mrs. Mardin, "while you were talking to Karl Krieg. I got the impression that Krieg was trying to talk you into something and you didn't look too happy about it. Then you waved to Frank, who started coming over. When Krieg saw Frank approaching, he quickly walked away. It was obvious that Frank was ready to beat Krieg's brains in, even there, and Krieg knew it. What was it all about?"

Joan Mardin spoke up. "Krieg was trying to con me. Said he had come to do me a favor. He offered to give us a lot of work."

"A piece of the Muni Yard Project?" I asked. "But it hadn't been awarded yet."

"Not a piece—all. Krieg was always selling hot air," Joan said. "Besides, with us doing the construction, our reputation would help him win."

"All the construction?"

"One hundred percent. For forty-nine percent of the profit. With Krieg's people deciding what's profit and what isn't. Using our payment and performance bonds and our credit and our laying out the payroll and the fringes and the union dues and you name it, with Krieg controlling who gets paid when. Including us. There's more to it than that, but that'll give you an idea of a typical Krieg deal."

"Have you told this to Moshe Gur?"

"Not about this job; what's the point with Krieg dead? But Gur knows all about some of the other Krieg deals," Joan said. "The worst part is, we were preparing to try for the Muni Yard our-selves."

"You were?" I sipped my drink and raised an eyebrow.

"Yes. The right way. We had our architects and engineers working on the project from the day it was announced. They were going to analyze everything until we were convinced that we could do it within the stated parameters, and we spent a lot of time and money on this phase of the work."

Frank took over. I noticed that they operated with the smooth rhythm of a long- and happily-married couple. "After we knew we could do the job, we approached Bevvy Benson to handle the fil-ings and papers, and she told us she was too busy. We knew what that meant: Karl Krieg. He had ignored the proper preliminary work, got some foreign investors to back him, and wanted to take a free ride on somebody else's back. Like on ours."

"So you had reason to kill him?"

Frank blinked.

"Everybody who ever had anything to do with him," Joan jumped in a little indignantly, "had a good reason to kill him. But nobody did, which is why he lived so long. Almost nobody."

"I think," Frank spoke up, "that whoever did it deserves a medal, and I'd be willing to chip in for it."

That said it all, as far as I was concerned. I announced, "I can see that there's no more useful information to get from this meet-ing, so let's enjoy our lunch."

"That sounds like a good idea," Frank said, reaching for an-other roll.

"Just one more thing," I said, remembering something. I looked at Joan. "Karl Krieg had the reputation of being a sex ma-niac, of going after every woman he met. Did he proposition you?"

"Not at the wedding," Joan said hesitantly. She set her roll on the white porcelain plate and looked down at it.

"You never told me." Frank's face was red.

"I was thinking of your blood pressure," his wife told him re-luctantly, finally looking up. "It was just the one time, when I first met him. I explained to him that if he would be kind enough to meet me in some dark corner and drop his pants, I'd be glad to remove the source of his stupidity with my specially sharpened Swiss Army knife. He hasn't bothered me that way since."

"Good for you," I said, then cleared my throat and asked, "Uh, do you carry that knife with you at all times?"

"If you're asking did I bring it to the wedding," Joan said, "the answer is, of course not. We've been in City Hall on business so many times, Frank and I, that we know the routine."

With that, the waiter showed up, bearing our lunches, and I focused most of my attention on digging into the succulent grilled lamb.

Back in my office, I finally had time to open the envelope of pictures Don O'Sullivan had given me. I flipped through them several times, knowing I would need a big block of time in order to really study them, but hoping something would jump out at me now.

Nothing did.

Finally, with a sigh, I tucked them into my briefcase and reached for the phone.

Ruth Gur answered on the second ring, efficient as she was beautiful.

After I identified myself, I leaned back in my leather chair and said, "I hate to bother you, Mrs. Gur, but I have to talk to you."

"Is anything wrong?" she asked, sounding distressed.

"You mean with Moshe? Certainly not. What I want is to ask you some questions about the murder in the chapel. I have an appointment in a few minutes, but after that I have some time. Can you be ready in a half hour? I'll send a limo to pick you up."

She hesitated. "The children will be here at three, so I can't come today. Will tomorrow be acceptable? Or better still, can— As long as we're on the phone, ask me now."

"Why not? Please don't worry, Mrs. Gur, it's just routine. Where were you sitting during the wedding ceremony?"

"In the middle of the section on the left. I tried to get aisle seats so that Moshe could find me easily, but some people were pushing so hard that I couldn't get anything on any aisle, so I took what was available."

"How long was it before your husband found you?"

"Not long, two or three minutes."

"Could your husband murder anybody?"

"You've known him for almost four years, Mr. Mayor," her voice was cold. "You may also have a Bible in City Hall. Read the Ten Commandments and answer the question yourself."

"You're right," I said, "and I apologize. I'll change the question. Could Moshe *kill* anybody?"

"Of course he could. Even I could. If anyone were to try to hurt the children, or me, he might, depending on the circumstances. He was a commando in the Israeli Army when I was in the infantry, and in defense of his country . . . And now that we're American citizens, anyone who tried to hurt America . . . Or if he saw a violent crime being committed and there was no other way to stop the attacker . . . Any decent human being can kill under the right conditions. Including you, Mr. Mayor," she added pointedly, apparently regaining her composure.

"One last question. Did Karl Krieg make any sexual passes at you?"

"You would have known if he had by the screams. His."

"Thank you, Mrs. Gur," I said, and hung up. An absolutely truthful answer and one I really didn't want to hear.

I was surprised to find out that Moshe had been a commando and wondered if there was anything more I didn't know about him.

Ken Lang still hadn't called me back, so I left another message, this time with his assistant, who said Mr. Lang was out of the office for the afternoon but promised to pass the word along.

I checked my watch and my schedule and saw that it was time to go to my appointment, which was in the press room. I was going to present an award to the Empire State Building elevator operator who had delivered those premature twins last week.

I stopped at Rosemary's desk on my way.

"Rosie," I said, "would you do me a favor and cancel my budget meeting for later this afternoon? You can reschedule it for tomorrow morning . . . I had set aside some time to work on my speech to the sanitation workers, but I can do that over the weekend."

Rosemary nodded and jotted a note on her pad.

"Then," I told her, lowering my voice and looking over my shoulder, "I want to see Vinnie Lobosco at my office as soon as possible. Tell him to be driven there, since it's him I want this time, and not the car."

Vinnie was in my office before I was. He must have been training his drivers himself.

"Don't sit down," I told him. "I need to pick your brains and I want to walk as we talk."

"*You* want to pick *my* brains? You're the brain around here."

"I don't have your . . . shall we say, *experience,* Vinnie." I led him out of my office and we started down the long corridor that's lined with oil portraits of former city officials. "Here's the problem. Remember the wedding last Sunday where a guy got stabbed?"

"Sure; it was on TV. Big mystery, huh? I guess they haven't caught whoever did it."

"Now do you remember what you used to do before I got you off on the murder charge?"

He looked at me suspiciously. "I was never arrested for nothing."

"But there were things you knew? Things you might have picked up from some accomplices—acquaintances—of yours?"

Vinnie was silent until we had passed through the waist-high wrought iron security gate, which an officer held open for us.

As soon as we were out of earshot and on our way down the carpeted center of the rotunda, he said, "You can't help hearing things, but who knows if it's just talk, or what."

"Exactly." We came to the metal detector located at the main entrance. I introduced him to the officer in charge.

"Mr. Lobosco wants to study how these new detectors work," I informed him.

"These babies," the officer said to Vinnie, "will pick up a dime under six layers of clothing, sir."

We watched for a few minutes as people came in and went out. Everything seemed to be working perfectly.

"Are these the same units that are used at the basement entrance?" I asked.

"All the units are the same, Mr. Mayor," the officer said.

"All the units in City Hall show on the first floor monitors bank?"

"They sure do."

"And how long are the tapes held?"

"For only a week—otherwise we'd need another building just for the tapes."

I thanked him and took Vinnie to the central monitor bank. The screens were small, but very sharp and clear. We watched for a few minutes, then went downstairs to the basement.

No one was coming in through the basement entrance, so we experimented by my emptying my pockets of everything but a dime and walking through the detector. The buzzer sounded promptly and the meter needle swung over.

It was clear that no one had carried the dagger through the metal detectors.

I then took Vinnie into the chapel, walking him around and giving him a verbal description of where everything was. I showed him where my suspects had been at about the time of the murder and, lastly, I showed him the alcove where the murder had taken place.

"How do you think he was lured here?" I asked Vinnie, stepping back and pointing at the alcove.

"That part's easy. Somebody gave him a come-on—sex, money, drugs, something—to get him to step in here. Once he was in, there was hardly any room to move, so the killer came in alongside, put his hand over the guy's mouth, stuck in the shiv, moved it a little, then let the body down quietlike. A few seconds and nobody'd notice, especially if they're all watching the front of the place."

"That's exactly what I figured, and the police, too, I'm sure. But who?"

"The guy who brought the knife in. Or the guy who helped him bring the knife in."

"But how did they do it?"

Vinnie looked around. "Any windows in any of the rooms down here?"

"None. Solid walls."

"Any dumbwaiters or some other way to get something from one of the other floors to down here?"

"None."

"Any mail chutes or pipe holes, chases, whatever you call them? Anything that goes from one floor to the basement?"

"Plenty of pipe chases, but they're all behind walls, and the police found no walls opened even a tiny bit."

"Any places to stash the knife?"

"Hundreds, but every single one was checked the morning of the wedding. Also, the movements of the guests in the hall outside the chapel were monitored and recorded."

Vinnie thought for a while, then told me, "Sorry, Mr. Koch; I can't do it. Maybe—if you want me to—I could find somebody who is more of an expert in this sort of thing . . ."

Quickly, I said, "No, thank you, Vinnie; you did very well." There was no way I was going to owe a favor to somebody who was more experienced than Vinnie at anything.

Back in my office, I summoned Moshe Gur, who showed up within minutes.

When he sat down in front of my desk, I told him I had spoken to his wife.

"You what? Why?"

"I told you I might have to, Moshe. Don't worry, I was gentle."

"Yeah, but Mayor—"

"She told me," I cut in, "that she had been in the infantry."

"At eighteen," he said, "all the boys and girls, except the ultra-Orthodox, go into the army for two years."

"She also told me you were a commando."

"It's on my record, and it's not a crime; it's something I'm proud of."

"You look soft, but you know many ways to kill."

"It's part of my training, sir." Gur was suddenly getting very formal with me. He even sat differently now, more rigid, his back not touching the chair.

"The Ten Commandments say 'Thou shalt not kill.' "

"No, they say 'Thou shalt not commit murder.' "

"So it's all right to kill under certain circumstances?"

"Of course. Self-defense, defense of your family, defense of your country, things like that."

I had to keep pressing. "How about killing an evil man to prevent him from committing a crime against your city?"

"It isn't permitted to kill a man such as Karl Krieg; you must depend on the laws of your country to punish him."

"If you have evidence against the murderer of Karl Krieg, would you give it to me?"

"I would, but I have no such evidence. And if he were caught, I'd hope he got the lightest possible sentence."

I know how to deal with the difficult people of the world; I would even have found a way to deal with Karl Krieg, if he hadn't gotten himself killed. But how do you deal with a completely honest man like Moshe Gur?

Assuming he hadn't lied to me, of course . . . and that's something that killers have a tendency to do.

Late that afternoon, I sat at my desk, immersed in paperwork involving yet another legal fight the city was waging. I was just thinking that I should wrap things up so that I wouldn't be late for the charity benefit I had to attend in Brooklyn Heights tonight, when Rosemary buzzed me.

"I've got an urgent call for you, Ed," she said.

Ken Lang at last, I thought.

But Rosemary continued, "It's your father."

Uh-oh. Right now was exactly the wrong time for Pop to call from Florida with something urgent. I'm used to handling several crises at a time, but a family crisis on top of everything else that was going on would be too much.

I picked up and said, "Hello, Pop. How is everything?"

"How should things be?" he said cheerfully. "Terrible. Your mother's getting crazier every day, one of my pinochle players is in the hospital from overeating, the food is terrible and they serve very small portions, the golf course is too close to our apartment, the card room is too far from the house, and they guarantee six hurricanes this year minimum. And that's the good part. So how's by you?"

"The usual stupidities. I have a speaker of the City Council I could rent to Boca Raton for hurricane practice, every time I try to cut a useless program I have pickets accusing me of taking bread out of the mouths of whatever their favorite mouths of the month are. I have essentially no control over the Metropolitan Transit Association, the Health and Hospitals Corporation, the Triborough Bridge and Tunnel Authority, and all the other covered agencies, but I get blamed for everything they do. Aside from these and a few trivial other things like them, everything's okay."

"Good." Bernard Koch doesn't listen. It's not that he's deaf; it's that he's not interested in anything that might make him deviate from his chosen course. "Listen, Ed, we're coming back home on Friday."

My jaw dropped. "Back home? You *are* home. You have a nice condo in a beautiful, warm part of the world where the sun shines every day, palm trees, flowers, no snow, no ice, no muggers, everybody plays pinochle. What could be nicer?"

"Mom and I figured that, with the beautiful weather you've been having—we've read all about it in the papers—"

"What beautiful weather? It's terrible here." Far be it from me to knock my beloved city for anything but an emergency. "And anyway, what papers are you reading? The Boca Raton papers give New York weather?"

"Who reads foreign papers? I read papers from where I live, New York."

Uh-oh. I knew what that meant.

But all I said was, "You don't live in New York; you live in Boca Raton. You don't have an apartment in New York anymore; you have a condo in Boca Raton. And Boca Raton papers aren't foreign. Florida, where you live, is part of the United States."

"We're *vacationing* in Florida, Eddie; we *live* in New York."

"You visit New York for less than half the year, Pop. You usually come up in mid-May. If you spend six months here, the IRS will hang you."

"So we'll go back a few days earlier next fall. Don't argue. I read in the papers—the *real* papers—that you got a problem. You know how I am with problems. I take care of them like lightning. So I figured I'd come up and help you."

Just what I needed. But I knew from experience that there was no arguing with my father. "You're going to stay with Sophie, aren't you?" I asked, my mind racing. "You could play with the grandchildren."

"Are you crazy? I should commute like a commuter?"

"Scarsdale to Grand Central Station is a short ride."

"A New Yorker does not commute. A subway, okay; a train, never. Where were you brought up?"

"But where will you sleep?" As though I didn't know.

"With you."

"At my apartment in the Village?"

My father snorted. "Greenwich Village," he informed me, "is full of boys with long hair and girls with short hair."

"That was in the old days."

"So they got some new *meshugaas,* big deal. No, Mom and I are gonna sleep in Gracie Mansion. You know how your mother loves to stay there. You should hear her brag about it to all her friends. Can you arrange to have us picked up at La Guardia Friday afternoon?"

I sighed. "All right. Call Rosemary with the flight information that morning."

"I have it right here," he said cheerfully. "Transfer me over. See you Friday, Eddie. And don't you worry. Your old man is going to bail you out of the mess you're in."

ELEVEN

Thursday morning, the big news on the way to work was that the city was about to be slapped with yet another lawsuit. A firefighter from the Bronx had been fired after his superiors discovered he was moonlighting as a male stripper named Smokey Blaze, wearing—and, obviously, not wearing—his official uniform as part of his act.

Though the Smokey Blaze scandal was bound to mean more headaches for me, I knew that this was the kind of story the local news and tabloid reporters love even more than they love a good murder.

I still hadn't heard from Ken Lang, and the only messages waiting for me when I got into the office were from Frank DeLauria, the fire commissioner, and several of the city lawyers.

Before getting down to business, I tried Ken Lang again, got his answering machine, and hung up on it, promising myself I'd call back later. No sense in leaving yet another message since he hadn't returned my others.

I buried myself in routine work, which I usually find boring as opposed to the public side of my job. But today, actually, it was a relief to surround myself with paper instead of people.

Just after nine o'clock, Rosemary put through a call from Lolly.

"I spoke to Ken Lang," she informed me as soon as I got on the line.

"You're kidding. I've been trying to reach him since yesterday."

"I know. He called me instead, figuring I'd know what you wanted to talk to him about."

"How did he sound?"

"Curious. Not particularly nervous, though, in case you were wondering," Lolly said.

"Did you tell him to get in touch with me?"

"Actually, I took the liberty of setting up an appointment with him and May, for eight-thirty tonight," she said. "That'll give them a chance to finish supper and we can have a leisurely dinner, too."

"No good," I said. "I want him hungry and tired and irritable. Make it for six."

"Six? Won't you be hungry, tired, and irritable, too?"

"Of course; that's the way an interrogation should be. I'll pick you up at five-thirty," I said, and went back to my soft, warm, boring work.

At six o'clock, Lolly and I were ushered into the Lang foyer by an obviously jittery May, who kept chattering about the wedding and about what a wonderful time Aileen and Alan seemed to be having on their honeymoon in Hawaii—they'd sent a crate of pineapples to the Langs just this afternoon, and wasn't that sweet?

Lolly and I agreed that it was, and followed May through the spacious first floor of their Murray Hill town house until we reached a large den that opened off the kitchen. It looked out over a courtyard, and through the wide-paned windows, I could see budding trees and blooming flowers.

Ken Lang was sitting there in an easy chair, looking hungry, tired, and irritable. He wore a maroon cardigan sweater and rumpled khaki pants, and behind his horn-rimmed glasses, there were deep circles under his eyes.

The only other furniture in the room, besides an enormous oak desk, was a couch that was on the same wall as the chair where Ken was seated.

There would be no easy way for me to look directly into his eyes

as I questioned him in this room, so after we had exchanged greetings, I suggested, "Why don't we talk in the kitchen?"

Without a word, May Lang led us back there, and Ken followed. On the counter, I noticed, was a big crate of pineapples,
marked "Fresh from the Aloha State."

I thought of Aileen and Alan. I sincerely hoped that they were
enjoying their honeymoon . . . and that they wouldn't come home
to find that one of their parents had been arrested for Karl Krieg's
murder.

I held a chair for Ken to make sure he'd sit where I wanted him
to and took a chair opposite him for myself.

I started the questioning in a roundabout way, with Lolly inter-
jecting pleasant little comments now and then. We talked about
the wedding, and about what a lovely bride and groom Aileen and
Alan were, and how happy they were going to be together, and
ya-da, ya-da, ya-da.

After a few minutes of this, I went in for the kill.

"You were alone and unobserved by any of the people we've
interrogated for a period of over three minutes while Krieg was
being killed," I told Ken. "What were you doing during that
time?"

He looked gray. "Nothing. Just standing there."

"Where is 'there'?"

"I was talking to Lolly in the corner—it was on the right side of
the room in the back—in the corner of the room for a long time. I
didn't check, but it was at least fifteen minutes."

"That was very close to where Karl Krieg was murdered."

"Look," he said, sounding irritated, "I've gone over all this
twice with the police. Do I have to go over it a third time with
you?"

"No, but if you don't, you may have to go over it a third time
with someone less friendly." Bluff, but it worked.

He folded. "I still don't know exactly where Krieg was killed,
but let's say it was near where I was standing with Lolly. What
does that mean?"

"By itself, nothing much. But Lolly left you about three minutes before the ceremony started, and no one remembers seeing
you for part of that time."

"I was walking over—actually pushing over; there were a lot of people in the way—toward the entrance, to May, to get ready for the ceremony."

"It would've taken you only two or three seconds to kill Krieg; no one would've noticed the missing few seconds and you would've come to the center aisle in plenty of time."

"There must've been twenty people or more who were in roughly that same position who didn't have to be anywhere."

"But none of them swore he'd kill Karl Krieg."

His eyes jumped to his wife, then quickly back to mine. "Where'd you hear that?"

"From a reliable source. I gather you haven't told that to the police."

"I never said it."

"I can be back tomorrow with the police and the reliable source, a lie detector, and a warrant for your arrest. Should I leave now?"

He took a deep breath. "No, I said it, but I didn't mean it the way it sounds. What I mean is . . . Sometimes people say things, like when they're angry, that they don't mean literally. Like even to the people you love. Haven't you ever said something like that?"

"Of course; we all have. But when someone turns up dead a few days later, and you're right there, and you're missing for the few seconds it would take to kill that someone, it could end up very badly for you."

"Are you going to tell Sergeant Deacon? I know he's in charge of the investigation."

He almost looked ready to cry, but I couldn't let myself feel too sorry for him.

Still, I softened my tone when I said, "I only tell Deacon things on a need-to-know basis."

"So does he need to know this?"

"Not as of now. Provided you tell me what Krieg did to you that made you wish him dead. I mean, you're an accountant, and not his accountant, so what could he do to you?"

For the first time this evening, Ken Lang's face became animated. Not pleasantly either.

"Karl Krieg cheated me in my own profession!" he burst out.

"He cost me three hundred thousand hard-earned dollars, not to mention the IRS interest and penalties, plus the lawyer, plus the time I lost from work, plus the sleep I lost, plus the way everyone in our association laughed at me behind my back."

"How is that possible? You're an accountant."

May Lang broke in. "Ken is getting all upset," she said. "I know the whole story, so I'll tell it."

Ken bristled. "May, I can—"

"No, Ken, let me," she insisted, and went on. "It was ten years ago, when Ken had a really good year and tax shelters were all the rage. Not that tax shelter is the right name; all it does is defer taxes for a few years so you can invest the money and later, if you have a bad year, you can take the money and pay taxes on it, but maybe in a lower bracket."

"Meaning . . . ?" I prodded.

"One of the ways is to join a group that's drilling for oil wells in a good area. You buy a large piece of land and divide it into, say, nine equal-sized square pieces making a square three pieces on a side. You get geological reports from independent, well-known experts, and everything looks like you'll make a lot of money in addition to the deferral of taxes for several years. Then you start drilling. So how can you lose?"

It was obvious to me, and to Lolly too, I could see by her face.

"I take it," I said, "that Karl Krieg was the one who sold you those shares of land."

May nodded. "He said to take our time, to check the reports for the land and the parcels we were buying as well as the surrounding area, check the bona fides of the experts, bring in our own geologist, whatever we wanted. If there were any shares left by that time, he'd gladly sell them to us at the quoted price. I want to emphasize that Ken discussed all this with me before we decided to buy the one share. Not that we couldn't afford it, but I would much rather have given Alan and Aileen that money to help them buy a house and start a family."

"Who decided where to drill the first well?" Lolly asked the key question.

"Karl Krieg," Ken burst out, obviously no longer able to contain himself, "the no-good crooked bastard. The first, second, third, and fourth wells, in the corners of the central parcel he'd kept for himself. No other wells. All the oil under our land was flowing into Krieg's wells. He made a fortune, and there was nothing we could do about it.''

I thought about that. "There have been similar cases—and here it would be easy to show intent—where the original investors recouped their money as well as their legal fees and other losses. Do you have the names of the other seven investors?''

"Of course," May said. "Ken did everything in a businesslike manner. Only how do you protect yourself against a crook like Krieg? And what do you do now that he's dead?''

"You can sue the estate," I said. "Lolly is more likely to know the right law firm than I am. Check with her next week. Meanwhile, Ken, I've decided not to tell Sergeant Deacon anything you haven't told him, and I won't . . . unless you're the killer.''

When Lolly and I were back in the limo, I told her I wanted her to make an appointment to see Mrs. Donna Krieg.

"Why do I have to do it?" she asked reluctantly.

"Because you've actually met her several times, haven't you?''

"Maybe once or twice, at fund-raisers. But Ed, come on. The woman must still be in mourning. Can't it wait till next week?''

"I doubt very much she's in mourning. Would you be, if you were married to a bastard like Krieg?''

Lolly thought that over, then said, "I'm not making any promises, but I'll call her—I can get the number from Bevvy—and see how she sounds.''

"Good. We'll take her to lunch, but make sure it's very early in the afternoon.''

"Why?''

I sighed. "I have a lot to do at the office before I can get out of there tomorrow night, and my folks are flying in.''

"Uh-oh.''

Lolly has met my parents on more than one occasion, and she knows how they are. Somehow, she tolerates them remarkably well—better than I ever have, especially when Pop gets started telling me how to run the city, and what I'm doing wrong.

"Isn't it awfully early in the year for them to be back from Florida?" Lolly asked.

"My father says he's coming to bail me out of this mess involving the murder . . . as if he can actually do anything to help."

"I think Bernie's cute."

"You're not his son."

"Who knows, Ed. Maybe he'll have some insight for you."

"That'll be the day."

"You never know. If you're going to find out who killed Krieg—and keep yourself in the good graces of the voters—you need all the help you can get."

Much as I hated to admit it, she had a point.

_____ TWELVE

Lolly called first thing Friday morning and said that she had made reservations for three at noon at Sur La Plage, a trendy, fairly new French restaurant in the East Sixties, off of Park.

I frowned. "Why there?"

"Donna picked it. Said it's one of her favorite places, and I figured it would be a good idea to have her in familiar surroundings."

"But I just ate French food on Wednesday," I grumbled. "What are you trying to do, kill me? And anyway, I'm more in the mood for Chinese."

"How can you say that at eight-thirty in the morning? At this hour, all I'm in the mood for is strong, hot black coffee," Lolly said.

"I'm always in the mood for Chinese," I pointed out, which was the truth. "But I guess this place will be fine, since it was Donna's idea. How'd she sound?"

"A little dazed. I think she's still in shock over Krieg's death."

"Nah," I said promptly. "You probably just woke her up when you called. A woman like Donna Krieg is probably used to sleeping till noon every day."

"Oh, sure, and eating bonbons, too, right?" Lolly asked sarcastically. "Ed, as I told you before, she *might* be in mourning, you know. The woman hasn't even been a widow for a week."

"And I told you to look at who she was married to," I shot back. "You can't honestly think she loved Krieg. I bet even his own mother couldn't stand him."

Apparently, Lolly couldn't argue with that, because all she said was, "See you at noon," before hanging up.

The widow Krieg was not wearing black—which showed integrity and good taste considering whose widow she was—but neither was she wearing anything at all like the sexy red dress she'd had on at the Benson-Lang wedding.

Today, Donna was clad in a simple tan wool-jersey sheath that clung in just the right amount to just the right places. With it, she had on sheer flesh-color stockings, and brown, low-heeled shoes. Her makeup was almost invisible, and her hair hung loosely around her face.

From what I knew of her, she had to be close to thirty-five, but someone who didn't know either one of the two women might have guessed that Donna was Lolly's daughter who had inherited her beauty from her mother.

I had been held up at a ground-breaking ceremony for a new apartment tower in Hell's Kitchen, and by the time I got to the restaurant, Donna and Lolly were on what was clearly their second round of drinks. I figured this out because there were two lemon zests in the ashtray; my old deduction cells were still operating on high, which was a good sign, considering what was on the agenda.

I introduced myself to Donna, even though she obviously knew who I was, shook her hand, and sat down.

The waiter was at my side immediately, asking what I wanted to drink in a phony French accent.

"A martini," I ordered, "made with Tanqueray gin and Martini and Rossi dry vermouth in a twelve-to-one ratio, neither shaken nor stirred, just swirled around in the glass, and one pearl onion, all in a prefrozen glass."

If James Bond can do it, I thought, *so can I.*

The waiter, looking slightly taken aback, nodded and disappeared.

I looked around and saw, from the clientele and the pseudo day-on-the-Riviera decor, that this was a highly pretentious place, full of snobs.

"Isn't it wonderful?" Donna asked, following my gaze. "It's a top restaurant and half the staff is authentically French, including our waiter."

Not on your life, I thought, but kept my mouth shut.

"I eat here regularly. I can get a table whenever I come in, and the food is very good."

"I'm sure it is," I lied.

The allegedly French waiter, who introduced himself as Marcel, showed up with my drink a few minutes later and asked whether we were ready to order.

I gestured at Donna. "Why don't you do the honors for all of us, since you come here often?" Might as well butter her up.

She looked pleased and turned to Marcel. She spoke to him in flawless French.

He replied with a little bow and a gracious, "Of course, Madame."

"What did you order?" I asked when he had made his exit. I hoped it was something filling . . . I was famished.

"I just told him to bring us whatever is the chef's specialty today. I also asked for small endive salads to start with, and said that we'll order dessert later."

"Where did you learn to speak French?" Lolly asked, clearly impressed.

"I studied in Paris for a year."

Lolly nodded and murmured, "Of course." But the look on her face betrayed her incredulity.

"You look surprised," Donna observed.

Lolly's cheeks glowed slightly. "I—er, not knowing anything about you other than that you were Karl Krieg's wife, and having met you only briefly a few times in passing, I had a different vision of what you'd be like."

"You thought I'd be a bimbo?" Donna responded, and it wasn't a question.

Lolly hesitated, then nodded. "Sorry, yes."

"Don't be embarrassed, Mrs. Winter; from the little you knew about me, I would've expected the same thing. I mean, what did you know? What did anyone know? That I was a showgirl in Vegas and that I was married to Karl Krieg. It's clear as day."

I jumped into the conversation. "Why don't you give us more information about yourself. Please. You're not obligated to do it, but it'll help us find who killed your husband. That is, unless . . ."

"I didn't do it," Donna said evenly, her lovely light green eyes meeting mine in a direct gaze. "But you probably don't believe me, Mr. Mayor—otherwise why would you be here?"

"I just want to ask you some questions. I'm trying very hard to find out who committed the murder."

"I'd like to know as much as you would," Donna said. "And believe me, I'm perfectly aware that I'm a popular suspect—and that the whole world knows there was no love lost between me and Karl."

"If it'll make you feel any better, you're the last one of the major suspects I've questioned."

"It doesn't make me feel any better about being on the list," Donna admitted, "but I guess anyone close to Karl would be under suspicion. I'll tell you what I told the police."

She looked around, as if to make sure no one was listening. The tables here were close together, though everyone around us seemed to be absorbed in their own conversations.

"Not much privacy here, is there?" Donna noted, turning back to Lolly and me. "I really should've invited you to eat at my place but . . . You'll understand later."

"Tell us now," I pressed.

Donna reddened a bit, then said, "I don't have any food in the house. Not for guests."

"You aren't much of a cook?" Lolly shrugged, as if to say, so what?

"No, of course I can cook. In fact, I was chef for the local diner when I was twelve years old, and nobody died from food poisoning." She hesitated, then added, "We were very poor. My father was killed in a car accident when I was twelve—they said he was drunk—and my mother had to take care of me and my little brother."

"Where were you living at that time?" I asked.

"In a little town near Nelson, about fifty miles south of Las Vegas. My mother worked, too, but my brother was too young. I didn't neglect school; at the diner I cooked early breakfast before school and then from after school till after supper. Then I went home and helped pick up around the house, did my homework, and went to sleep. No friends and no social life; I was a tall, scrawny, ugly kid."

"*You?*" I couldn't help saying it that way, considering the dazzling woman sitting opposite me.

"I'm not making this up; it really hurt. Nobody wanted to know me till I was sixteen when all of a sudden, every boy in the school, in town also, was after me. Men too."

"How'd you handle it?" Lolly asked.

"Same way you probably did, Mrs. Winter."

Probably not the same way, I thought, from what I occasionally overheard when Lolly and Bevvy were whispering about their college days.

"The way I felt about those boys was, you didn't like me the way I was then, but I'm the same person now, only shaped a little different on the outside. So why should I have believed they really liked me all of a sudden? After a while, they got the idea and left me alone. Besides, I wanted to go to college, not beauty culture school like some of the girls in my class."

"And, obviously, you did go to college," I said.

She nodded. "I got a partial scholarship to the University of Nevada. I knew I'd have to get a good-paying job that would leave my days open. That's when I wandered into a big casino, figuring I could get a job as a dealer, night shift. I have a good head for numbers—I also did the diner's bookkeeping—and I was sure that in one week, maybe less, I could learn to be their best dealer. I did, eventually."

"And then you went to France to study?"

"For a year, yes," she said, nodding. "And when I got back to Vegas, I couldn't get my job back at the casino."

"And that's when you became a showgirl?" Lolly asked.

"Exactly. I didn't want to—the way I was brought up on the Bible, it was sinful for a woman to go around half-naked and tempt men—but the pay was great, I didn't go around naked, I had beautiful costumes, and the work was easy. Also I had the right qualifications; all you had to do was be very tall, very beautiful, have big boobs, and move gracefully through some easy dance routines."

I had a sudden vision of Smokey Blaze and the lawsuit he'd filed against the city. There was a lot waiting for me back at the office. I decided I needed to step up the pace of this interrogation.

"Anyway," Donna was saying, "I made a deal with one of the other girls to share an apartment with her—I'd do all the shopping, cooking and cleaning, keep on top of all the bills, hers and ours, and pay one-quarter of the rent and utilities—so I could send part of my earnings home to my mother. I still send her some money— at least up till now—and also something to my brother, who has a big family and doesn't make much of a living."

I decided to get Donna back on track with a polite verbal nudge. "May I ask," I said when she paused for a moment, "why you—"

The waiter chose that moment to bring the endive salad, and I clamped my mouth shut. There was silence for a moment while we tasted it. It was, I was pleased to discover, absolutely perfect.

I wanted to get the momentum of the questioning going again, and I still had a lot of work piled up in my office, so I asked, "Where did you meet Karl Krieg—and why did you marry him?"

Donna blushed. "Before I was sixteen, when no boy would even hold my hand, I saw what happened to my classmates. Some of them ended up in real big trouble, the kind of trouble I couldn't afford to have, and a few of them even got engaged, before graduation, to some of the creepiest boys in town, boys you wouldn't want to live in the same state with, much less be married to."

"Boys that would grow up to be like your deceased husband?" I asked.

"Exactly like him, and you could tell that a mile off. But Karl wasn't always fat and he wasn't always bald. When I first met him in a casino that night, and the next few days, he was polite and thoughtful and interesting and fun. . . . How was I to know it was all an act? I could tell that kind of bull from the kids I knew, and even the men, but Karl was big-time, a pro, and what he wanted, he usually got. And it was flattering that a much older, very successful businessman wanted me, and was willing to marry me to get me.

"Besides," she went on, "he had his moments. You know, he had a wonderful, almost childlike sense of humor. He loved to read the comics in the Sunday papers, and he loved to watch cartoons. And he showered me with attention. To tell the truth, I was flattered. My apartment mate—like all the other girls who were single—had a different man every night, and some of these guys were very generous with gifts."

"Karl too?" Lolly asked.

"Not gifts, promises. He would tell me about all the deals he was working on. Some of them were real clever and none of the ones he told me about were crooked. 'When we're married,' he'd say, 'I'll lay the world at your feet.' So we got married. It wasn't one week before he changed. Started insulting me, yelling at me, accusing me of marrying him for his money."

"Well, didn't you?" I asked.

She thought for a moment. "No, I didn't."

"Would you have married him if he didn't have any money?"

"No, but that's not the same thing, is it?"

"And you stayed with him," Lolly asked, "for sixteen years?"

"I couldn't get away. I never had money. I could use a credit card until the limit was reached, then I had to use a different card and so on. He never paid a bill unless he was forced to. I can't go into half the shops in New York. I never was allowed to see any bills or checks. He doled out the money I was allowed. I never had more than twenty dollars in my bag. Which is why I have no food in the house, by the way. I mean, I'm not starving, but it's no fun to eat farina three times a day."

The waiter came with a thick slice of truffled paté and some melba toast. "Compliments of the chef, Madame," he told Donna, who dug in after Lolly had taken a small sliver and I had done the same.

When the last bit of paté was gone, I said, "With all Karl's money, you don't have enough for groceries?"

"He never used cash and never kept cash in the house."

"So where did he keep it? Or the bankbooks? Records? There had to be something."

"He kept everything in his head. Maybe a few notes in his own code, but nothing I could figure out."

"You checked his papers?" Lolly asked.

"Pried open his desk—I'm the only possible heir, so it was all right—but what I found was useless."

"So you'd be rich, if you could find out where he hid the money?"

"Very, but if he could keep it hidden from the Internal Revenue Service—he really hated them—there's no way I can find it now."

I thought of something. "At the wedding, Karl supposedly had an envelope with him, full of money."

Donna smiled sadly. "That wasn't money; it was newspaper. He made me cut it up."

Good old Karl Krieg. Even when he was doing something crooked, he had to do it crookedly.

Lolly asked, but it really wasn't a question, "I take it Karl was also fooling around?"

"Right after our wedding, I found out that he had made a pass at my ex-roommate—who advised me to ditch him as soon as possible—and a day later I heard from a reliable source that he'd been seen coming out of a motel room with a known prostitute. When he came back to our honeymoon suite, half-drunk, I accused him of that. He passed it off as normal, told me that I was a cold fish, and if I didn't shut up, he'd spoil my face for good."

"Why did you stay?"

"I don't know. Partly because I had been brought up that marriage was for life, partly because I didn't want to fail, partly because I thought that maybe it was my fault, that maybe if I became more loving . . . I don't know. Whatever it was, I stayed with him for a year before I decided that there was nothing wrong with me, that everything was wrong with him. But then it was too late."

"Why was it too late?" I asked, just as the waiter trundled out a huge cauldron of bouillabaisse.

He had terrible timing, I decided, as he set big bowls on the table, with knives, forks, oyster forks, and spoons, along with a gravy boat of aioli sauce. Donna told him that we would serve ourselves, and he nodded and retreated—no doubt plotting a return the next time I asked the widow Krieg a provocative question.

Donna heaped our bowls with the savory shellfish, and dug into hers with such gusto that I didn't have the heart to interrupt her with a topic that would turn anyone's stomach: her late husband.

So, for the next fifteen minutes or so, we merely ate and made the occasional chitchat about the weather—which was perfect—and the food—which was the same.

Finally, when Lolly and I had finished our first helpings and Donna had put away her second, I said pointedly, "I don't mean to bring up an unpleasant subject again, Mrs. Krieg, but why is it that you couldn't leave your husband?"

"It's simple," she said promptly. "Staying with Karl was the only way I could make sure my mother and my brother were taken care of."

"That's very admirable of you," I said, and I meant it. Still, we were here on business, so I asked, "Were you near your husband when he was killed?"

"I don't know exactly when he was killed," she said, "but I'm pretty sure I wasn't near him at any time after we came in. Remember that red dress I was wearing?"

"Who could forget?"

She blushed. "I've been better covered than that on stage in Las Vegas. Karl bought it and made me wear it. I was supposed to attract Moshe Gur and soften him up for Karl to work on. Crazy. The man wears a yarmulke, so he's Orthodox. I'm sort of Orthodox myself—not Jewish, but I know what Orthodox people stand for—and his wife is in the room and I'm wearing a dress you could see from a mile away. Karl must've been desperate to do that. Anyway, I talked to Gur for about thirty seconds before he excused himself. He was polite, but I could see he thought I was the Whore of Babylon. As far as I could tell, Karl was dead with Moshe Gur from that moment on—he didn't have a chance in hell of getting the big job."

"So where was your husband at that time?"

"I have no idea. When he aimed me at Gur, he said not to look for him, that he'd be working the room and to forget about him. So that's what I did, and I didn't worry that he wasn't sitting next to me during the wedding service. Which was pretty good for a civil ceremony, by the way."

I chose to take that as a compliment and thanked her.

There was nothing else to ask.

When the waiter came for our dessert order, he mentioned the chocolate velvet cake: a hemisphere of chocolate fondue covered with a thin layer of gâteau covered with a frosting of glossy chocolate. With a big chocolate bow and a generous helping of whipped cream on top.

"That sounds yummy!" Donna said, practically clapping her hands in delight. "We'll take three. With extra whipped cream."

I sincerely hoped she wasn't the killer.

THIRTEEN

A luxurious, if too pretentious for my taste, restaurant promotes leisurely dining, and with the questioning of Donna Krieg, I had spent nearly two hours at midday on nonofficial business.

As a result, it was well after six before I completed the minimum number of meetings and the required amount of paper reading and signing.

The Smokey Blaze dispute showed every sign of becoming an enormous nuisance. Of course, the press had gathered on the steps of City Hall to fire questions at me regarding the case as I left. I obliged until someone brought up the murder; at that point, I beat a hasty retreat to the limo.

On my way to dinner at Gracie Mansion, I had the driver stop to pick up Lolly, who had invited herself along for tonight. For some reason, she finds my parents charming.

As soon as we stepped into the foyer of Gracie Mansion, Bernard and Lillian Koch pounced on us.

Pop beamed when he saw Lolly and she beamed when he beamed.

I shook my father's hand, kissed my mother's cheek, and asked how she felt with her new artificial knee, which she'd obtained through an operation just before the holidays.

"It's wonderful, Eddie. I'm learning folk dancing," she said, rolling up the leg of her lavender slacks to show it off.

"Is folk dancing such a good idea, at your age, Ma?"

"What else do you want me to do? Watch him play pinochle all day long?"

"You have to be careful," I said. "Some of those dances can be pretty strenuous. Don't overdo it."

"It's like I always say," she said. "Anything worth doing is worth overdoing."

"Like at the airport?" Pop asked. "Those things are made for terrorists."

"What things?" I asked.

"Those metal detectors. And your mother, does she tell the attendant about her new knee? No. Not a word. The buzzer goes off, she's carrying nothing, the attendant wants to go over her with the hand-thing, and what does she do? She makes a big fuss."

"I'm an American citizen," Lillian Koch said. "I pay my taxes; I'm entitled."

"Next time you cause a scene," Pop said, "I'm getting on the plane without you and I'll give the pilot a good tip to take off fast."

My father, the former waiter, firmly believes that a good tip is the key to obtaining most things in life. Actually, he might have a point.

"Hmmm. I can see," Lolly said dryly, catching my eye, "that Edward has inherited certain qualities from both of you."

"From who else?" Pop said. "Okay, enough talk; let's eat."

I started taking off my trench coat.

Pop stopped me with a hand on my arm. "What do you think you're doing, Eddie?"

"Getting ready to eat?" I suggested patiently; after all, Pop *is* getting up there in years, and he'd had a long day, with all the traveling.

"For that you put your coat on."

"We're going to eat with our coats on?"

"No," he said with exaggerated patience, "we go *out* with our coats on and when we get there, we *eat* with our coats off."

"When we get where?"

"The Merkin Deli, of course. I just spent a six-month winter vacation down in Florida, where they wouldn't know even a medium good pastrami if it bit them, and you want me, when I finally come back home, not to have my first meal in New York at the only deli in town that knows how to make a perfect pastrami on rye with caraway?"

This was not an argument I could win. My father had been the number one waiter at the Merkin all of his life. Why should he have to, on his first night back in New York, eat food prepared by my very expensive personal four-star chef, who was not a pastrami maven?

Stifling a sigh, I put my coat back on.

The Merkin Deli, like every real deli in New York, is not pretentious.

The tabletops are mottled gray plastic with chromed edging, the chairs are simple, slightly padded wood, the lights are lights, and the wall across from the counter is solidly mirrored. The flooring is made of soft mottled gray tiles and the ceiling is beige acoustic tile.

The tables are barely far enough apart for a skinny waiter to get through and if you want a fork, you have to ask for it; this is a sandwich shop, a two-handed sandwich shop. In fact, just asking for a fork or a knife—a spoon for your soup is okay—shows that you're from some foreign land such as Staten Island or New Jersey.

The deli is a short walk from the Merkin Concert Hall and a slightly longer walk from Carnegie Hall. When we arrived, a few latecomers were frantically trying to get the tables that the conscientious and prudent music lovers were slowly and reluctantly leaving. Holding the barbarians at the gate was, as usual, little gray Sol—last name unknown—who still looked old enough to be my grandfather.

He took one look at my father, said, "Bernie! I've been holding the comics table open for you," like he'd just seen my father yesterday, and led us to a table in the near corner of the shop.

I had no doubt that if I had come there without my father, I would've had to wait with everyone else.

When the waiter came over—they all looked so young compared to what I'd been used to when my father brought me here as a boy—Pop ordered four perfect pastramis on seeded rye without consulting the rest of us.

"Any really good deli," Pop informed Lolly after the waiter had left, "knows how to make a good corned beef. A few even know how to make a perfect corned beef, as good as you could get here. A very small number can make a very good brisket, and of that number, maybe two could make a brisket as good as the Merkin does. But pastrami?"

He paused for effect, and punctuated the silence with a resounding *crunch* into a sour pickle.

"There's no secret as to how to make pastrami in this town," he continued. "It's all in the perfect ingredients, the perfect spices, and the care you take, the feel for when the right moment has been reached, the way it's cut, how the sandwich is assembled. . . . A bunch of little things, like the exactly right amount of pickle juice in the mustard and the quality of the bread. Back in my day, I was proud to serve a pastrami on rye here. Not everyone could make it."

Lolly asked him how he'd come to work here, and that got Pop going.

My mother and I exchanged a glance that said, "Now look what she's started."

In record time, the waiter brought over our sandwiches, mercifully interrupting one of Pop's long-winded stories about some old-time gangster he'd once served.

"Can I get you anything else?" the waiter asked.

Pop looked at the sandwich suspiciously, but didn't touch it. "Ask Sol to come over," he told the waiter. When the waiter disappeared, Pop motioned us all not to touch our sandwiches.

My mother and I exchanged another glance.

Sol came over, visibly disturbed. "What's the matter, Bernie?" he asked.

"Taste the sandwich," Pop said.

"Bernie, I picked out the pastrami personally when you phoned me you were coming."

"Taste the sandwich," Pop repeated.

Sol put on his glasses and peered closely at the sandwich. Suddenly he paled. "Machine sliced?" Pop nodded. "You asked for a perfect pastrami on rye?"

"Who knows better than me how to order? And on top of that, you see any caraway seeds? Even one seed?"

Sol snapped into action. He called the young waiter over and made him take the sandwiches away. Then he told him to make sure that the new sandwiches were hand-carved, that the bread had caraway seeds, and that the knishes were evenly browned.

Furthermore, he ordered that the four of us should have as much celery tonic to drink as we wanted, that the pickle bowl be kept filled, that there would be no bill, and if he got a tip, it would be only because of the undeserved generosity of Mr. Bernard Koch, who was the number one waiter at the Merkin when this waiter was still peeing in his diapers.

After the poor kid had slunk off into the back, Sol turned back to Pop and said, "It's the new young generation. They don't want to learn. In Europe, being a waiter is a profession, and respected. Here, it's for actors in between auditions."

"I know, Sol," Pop said. "It's like they think there's nothing to being a waiter. You breathe; you get paid for breathing. You half listen; that's all the lousy customer deserves. Somebody asks for a suggestion, you don't know good from bad because all you ever eat comes from the freezer or the toaster oven."

"You want to come back to work, maybe?" Sol asked hopefully.

"I can't, Sol," Pop said, "much as I'd like to. I got two guys in my winter vacation colony that think they're pinochle players, even though I got to explain to them the difference between a king and a queen sometimes. Nobody else there knows how to play pinochle. Without me, their wives would make them take up folk dancing and they'd die."

"Hey!" my mother said, and nudged his arm.

Pop wasn't fazed. "But, Sol, I'll tell you what I'll do. I'm going to spend the next week or so with Eddie—call me at Gracie Mansion—and after that with my daughter Sophie in Westchester—I'll leave you her phone number. If you ever get stuck and you need me, give me a call and I'll come over."

Sol looked at my mother. "It's okay?" he asked.

"He's as strong as an ox," she said. "But no more than twice a week." She hesitated, then asked, "Any folk dancing groups around here?"

"Are you kidding? This is the dance center of the world. I'll see what I can find out for you, Lily."

The waiter brought the orders. We started eating. The sandwiches were perfectly perfect, the only problem being how to get your mouth opened wide enough to take a bite of the whole thickness of everything.

Lolly asked for a fork; clearly pastrami is not in her genes.

After the waiter had cleared the table, Lolly asked Pop, "Why is this called the comics table?"

"Because this is where the comics met when they were in town. They came here because the food is great, the price is right, and nobody bothers you in between the rush hours. It was like a meeting room for all the stand-up comics, and my table was the one they always sat at, because I was the best waiter of the best waiters in town."

"Oy," my mother said, and shook her head.

Pop ignored her. "Milton Berle, he knew even more jokes than Henny Youngman—or maybe it was the other way around. And then there was Red Buttons, Sid Caesar, Myron Cohen, Lou Holtz, Joe E. Lewis, Fat Jack Leonard, Buddy Hackett, Totie Fields, Rodney Dangerfield—only then he was called Jackie Roy— Willie and Eugene Howard, Jack Benny, the Marx Brothers, Larry Storch, the Ritz Brothers . . . I could go on and on. Woody Allen, when he was poor, came here. When he became a big star, he went to eat at the Russian Tea Room. Crazy. They don't know how to make a perfect pastrami on rye like the Merkin—borscht maybe; piroshki, maybe; but pastrami? No way. So what'd he go for?"

"I never could understand that myself," Lolly murmured politely.

"Well, it's getting late," I said, standing up, "and you must be tired from your flight . . ."

"Sit down," Pop said.

I sat.

"Now is the time to talk about your problem."

"Which problem, Pop?" I asked. "Being mayor of this city, I have a few, you know."

"The other problems are nothing; I'm talking about your being the prime suspect in a murder case. The murder of Karl Krieg."

"I am not a prime suspect in any murder case, and I want you to stop reading the tabloids, especially the gossip columns."

"You're telling me what I can read, now? The front-page stories in any paper are advertisements and come-ons for whatever dumb ideas whoever owns the paper wants to push. The gossip columns tell the truth, even if it can't be proved. And if you ever want to get reelected, you better pay attention to the gossip columns, because that's the one thing that everybody reads and believes."

Who was I to argue with that?

"Listen, Eddie," Pop said, "I'm just the right guy to help you. You'd be surprised what a waiter hears and can put together just from happening to overhear a few words here and there, even on different days. You wouldn't believe how many divorces I predicted when I was working, and how many business deals."

"Okay," I gave in; what else could I do? "I'll read the gossip columns. Now how are you going to help me?"

"First tell me everything—don't leave anything out—about the case."

So I did, keeping my voice down and keeping an eye on the people at the next table, who, though they were only about two feet away, were too busy arguing over their rice pudding to pay any attention to us.

When I was done explaining the case, Pop sat back and thought for a while.

"According to what you said, nobody could've done it," he finally concluded. "The prime suspects are all nice people, they all had motives but not really enough to kill Karl Krieg, and especially not in the City Hall Chapel. All of them were seen near the murder location by one or more people, there was no way to get hold of the murder knife, and there was a very short time—ten minutes at most, maybe less—during which the murder could've been committed."

"That's the problem," I said, in a *tell me something I don't already know* tone.

"So what you're saying is that nobody could've committed the murder. But a murder was committed. Therefore, somebody's lying. At least one of them, maybe all of them."

"Or someone we never suspected," I offered.

"No." Pop was firm. "From what you just told me, and from what I've read in the papers, it had to be one of those five suspects. I hope you appreciate that I'm leaving you off the list, Eddie."

"I love you, too, Pop."

"We have to start with being absolutely certain that every one of these people is lying."

"Bevvy doesn't lie," Lolly said. "I've known her since we were roommates in school and she's as straight as they come."

"That's Mrs. Benson?" Pop asked. "The mother of the bride?" Lolly nodded.

"So let me ask you some questions. When you were in school, you were what? Eighteen to twenty-two?"

"Twenty-three. We both went to graduate school."

"And Beverly Benson was the same age?"

"A year younger."

"And during those five years," Pop pressed on, "Beverly never lied to her mother?"

"Only when necessary . . . for her mother's own good."

"And she also lied to your mother, for you?"

Lolly blinked. "What makes you think that?"

"I wasn't born yesterday."

She hesitated, then admitted, "In emergencies only."

"And she never lied to the school administrators? To her professors? To other students?"

"Not very often."

"And to the boys?"

Lolly turned red. "You're supposed to lie to boys; they always lied to us."

Pop leaned back in his chair. "So your friend Bevvy is a liar. And so are you. And so am I. Everybody lies at some time. Everybody. They're all liars, these suspects, just remember that. Even Eddie."

I nearly spit out a huge mouthful of celery tonic. "Pop!"

"Remember when you were three, and you drew the Statue of Liberty on the kitchen wallpaper in crayon?"

"What does that have to do with lying?"

"You signed your sister Sophie's name to it. It's the same thing. You're a liar. Everyone's a liar. I assure you, if the police ever arrested me for murder, you'd hear some really good plain-and-fancy lying. Assuming I decided to say anything at all. I'd even lie to my own lawyer in a murder case."

"Admirable," I muttered.

Pop ignored me. "Now if Bevvy, who couldn't possibly lie, lied about the murder, you can be damn sure that the other four also lied. So all you have to do is talk to them again, catch one of them in a lie—even a small one—and use that as a wedge to crack the case wide-open."

"That's what I was trying to do the first time around," I said. "Everything I heard sounded true and made sense. It all fit perfectly with what I had learned from the other prime suspects. And I'm sure they were all cooperating fully."

Actually, I wasn't sure of that, or that everyone was telling the truth, but I didn't want to get into that with Pop.

I continued, "We—Lolly and I—had lunch with Mrs. Krieg today and I could swear that she was as nice a person as you'd ever meet. Right, Lolly?"

"That's how she came across, yes."

"Anyway, Pop, how do you get any of our suspects to lie so we can force them to talk?"

"First of all, don't get the idea that after you catch them once, and they talk, the second time is going to be the truth, the whole truth, and nothing but the truth. The next time it'll be another lie, a different lie. You got to keep the pressure on, and it doesn't hurt to lie a little yourself. Like maybe you tell them that you found out something, or you heard something, or one of their alibi witnesses admitted something. Whatever you need at the time you need it. You ever watch any of those real cop shows on TV, Eddie?"

"Most days I don't even have time to go to the toilet," I informed him bluntly.

He wasn't daunted. "They're very educational, those shows. Let me give you an example. Some drug dealer is driving down a highway in a panel truck. Inside the truck are various items he wouldn't want the cops to notice. Like, maybe, a bale of marijuana, ten kilos of cocaine, two thousand bottles of crack, a couple of submachine guns, and ten boxes of bullets. Suddenly he hears a siren behind him and the lights of the police cruiser that's been following him for the past mile are flashing like crazy. The police signal him to pull over. Does he make a run for it?"

"Only if he's crazy, Pop."

"Right. He pulls over. One of the cops in the cruiser gets out and politely asks him for his license and registration. The dealer smiles nicely and gives the papers to the cop. Why sweat; the papers are very good counterfeits. The cop goes back to his car and checks in his computer. Meanwhile, the other cop, with a flashlight, tries to look through one of the back windows of the panel truck. No good; they're painted solid."

"I'm not an armed cop," I said impatiently, "and the prime suspects aren't people who can be easily fooled."

"It's the technique I'm trying to teach you, not how to become a cop. Anyway, the first cop goes back to the dealer and tells him his rear light is out and he has to give him a ticket. The dealer smiles and says, 'Sure'—that's how relieved he is; doesn't give him the slightest argument like even old ladies do, or get out of the car to see if the light is really out. That, in itself, is very suspicious, but the dealer has no choice. Just like your suspects. If you ask the right questions, they got no choice either."

"Okay, fine. How do you know what the right questions are?" I asked.

"You're a politician and you have to ask?"

"That's different. There I know who the crooks are—my opponents."

Pop made a face and went on. "Meanwhile, the second cop comes up to the dealer's window, opens his holster, making sure it's a loud snap, and while he's looking hard past the dealer trying to see what's in the back, says, 'You got a flat tire in the back. Why don't you get out and look at it. We'll help you change it.' Any honest person would go out and look right away, especially if the cops offer to help change it."

"Come on, Pop, what's your point?"

"The dealer is sweating," he continued without missing a beat. " 'That's all right,' he says, 'I was getting off at the next exit anyway.' 'Okay,' says the first cop, 'we'll follow close behind you in case you have any trouble and my partner will call ahead to make sure you're taken care of properly.' He starts writing out the ticket. Slowly. To give the dealer time to sweat. Meanwhile the second cop is calling ahead with one hand and aiming the shotgun with the other. What does the dealer do?"

"He admits to a lesser crime."

"Exactly. Not that it'd help him in this case, which I actually saw on the TV—I don't play pinochle all the time, like your mother says—where he admitted that he had cigarettes without the tax stamps and pointed out that the state they were in doesn't consider untaxed cigarettes such a terrible thing and could he pay the value of the stamps directly right now and be on his way while the cops went to wherever they took the money to send to the state capital. Of course, that was the end—another charge and now they could search all they wanted."

"Something like that'll be a little harder to do with these suspects."

"So? I taught you to be afraid of hard work?" Pop asked, and motioned for another refill on his celery tonic, then leaned back in his chair and gloated.

FOURTEEN

Since no one in Gracie Mansion even knew what pinochle was, Pop insisted on coming with me to talk to Bevvy on Saturday morning.

That his son, the mayor, still needed him—at least, to his way of thinking—made it all the better.

To my way of thinking, now he would see how well the lecture he gave me the night before at the Merkin Deli worked in practice. Not that I wanted to see him fail, but maybe it was time for him to learn, even at his age, that not all problems have simple solutions and that his son, who had made it to mayor of New York practically on his own, was capable of solving, and had already solved, some really big problems.

Mom had found a folk dancing class that she could walk to at a Yorkville Senior Citizens Center. She had taken off early in the morning with her little cotton turquoise palm tree–imprinted beach bag—sure to look out of place here on the Upper East Side—and her dancing slippers.

"Careful on that knee," I warned her as she kissed me good-bye.

"You know, Eddie," she said, straightening my collar, "a couple of hours of dancing every day is exactly what you need to get that strained look off your face."

I was polite enough not to remind her that a strained look in private was normal for any mayor of New York City, even if he wasn't a prime suspect in a murder case, and that some of the strain came from parents who, with only two days' notice, came to New York weeks earlier than expected and took part of my concentration away from solving the case.

It was a nice day, so Pop and I decided to walk to Bevvy's apartment. I needed the exercise, and I always loved meeting the citizens of the city. I figured that with everything that was going on, it would be a good thing for me to be seen conducting business as usual.

Pop and I, with my bodyguards ahead and behind, walked south along York Avenue, with big luxury apartment houses on our right and FDR Drive, which edged the East River, to our left. The tiny waves on the water's surface flickered in the bright April sunlight.

Actually, the East River is not a river; it's a tidal strait that flows in one direction part of the day and in the opposite direction another part, in harmony with the tides of the Atlantic Ocean. When I was a boy, kids used to go swimming in it, diving off the piers that lined the banks.

"Yo, Ed!" called a young kid who passed us on the street, wearing slouchy clothes and a backward baseball cap.

"Yo," I returned with a wave. "How'm I doin'?"

"You're doin' all right, bro'."

"Who was that?" Pop asked as soon as he'd passed.

"I have no idea, Pop. I'm the mayor, remember? People recognize me."

"What, you don't know anybody in this town personally, Eddie?"

I gritted my teeth. "Yes, of course I do, but not that particular kid."

We kept walking, people kept greeting me, and every time, Pop asked me if I knew the person. By the time we were within a few blocks of Bevvy's, I regretted ever bringing him along, even if I had done it only to teach him a lesson.

"You're sure this Bevvy will be there?" Pop asked. "Saturday was always shopping day when I lived here."

"Still is, but not this early," I assured him. "Right now she's probably still dressed in a jogging outfit." We walked on a few steps, and I decided I had to say it. "Pop, please remember that she's a friend of mine, and she's Lolly's closest friend. We're not going to hammer her or treat her badly."

Pop looked insulted. "I always treat a lady like a lady."

I thought of the stories he used to tell of his Merkin Deli days. "And what about a lady who doesn't tip properly?"

He shrugged. "If she doesn't tip properly, she's no lady."

Bevvy was in simple sports clothes, and looking very nice for a liar.

"Would you like a drink?" she asked us after I introduced my father.

"A small one for me," I said. "Anything, but if you have it, Armagnac."

"A big one for me," Pop said. "Would you happen to have buffalo grass vodka?"

Bevvy looked surprised. "Why, yes, but hardly anyone ever asks for it or even knows it exists. Are you of Russian descent?"

"Polish," Pop said. "All the best Russian vodka is made in Poland."

Bevvy poured the three drinks—a light white wine for herself—and led us into a large study off the entry hall. The room's old-fashioned moldings and fireplace—not to mention the antique furniture including an enormous carved desk—looked slightly out of place next to an array of high-tech office equipment.

"I hate going to work on the weekends, so I'm fully connected here electronically, in case I'm needed," Bevvy explained. She took a sip of wine as we sat down in upholstered easy chairs.

"We also have privacy in the office," she added, which I took to mean that her husband wouldn't open the door without knocking.

Pop took a big slug of his vodka.

"I was wondering," I told Bevvy, sipping my brandy, "if you would mind replaying the tape of your conversation with Karl Krieg. I'd like to hear it again."

Bevvy narrowed her eyes slightly. "Why?"

"Because I want to make sure I didn't miss anything," I said truthfully.

She hesitated.

I watched her carefully, thinking that if she was as innocent as Lolly and I wanted to believe she was, she wouldn't have a problem with playing the tape again.

After a moment, Bevvy put her glass of wine down on the desk, took the tape from a drawer, and put it into the tape player. Without comment, she pressed play. Her voice—and Karl Krieg's— filled the room.

When the tape was finished, before I could open my mouth, Pop shook his head and said, "Boy, that Krieg was some bastard. And you're no innocent little shrinking violet either."

"Pop," I said in a warning tone.

"When somebody's trying to cheat you out of two million bucks," Bevvy said, "nobody's an innocent."

"I'm glad you said that," I told Bevvy, "because I have a question for you. Where's the rest of the tape?"

"That's the whole thing, Ed."

"He says 'See you at the wedding,' and that's all? No good- byes, no nothing?"

"You heard the sound of the phone being hung up."

"I heard the sound of one phone being hung up, a sound that would be easy to imitate by any phone. I didn't hear the sound of two phones being hung up while the tape was still running. Is it possible that you cut off the end of the tape yourself?"

"Aha!" Pop said, looking impressed with me.

I gave him another warning look and turned back to Bevvy.

She fiddled with her wineglass, rolling the stem back and forth in her fingers. "The tape is whole; what you heard is what happened."

"Look, Bevvy," I said gently, "I'll bet that in the police lab they have technicians who can tell if the tape's been cut short. And—"

"I could probably tell myself," Pop cut in, "just by buying a new tape and stretching it out and measuring one against the other. I'll bet the new tape is a little longer than the one you have in your machine."

"I doubt if tapes are made exactly to a certain length," Bevvy said. "In any manufacturing process, there are always small errors."

"Of course there are," I said, shooting Pop a glance that said *let me handle this.*

"Of course," Pop went on, ignoring me, "you can either tell us what was missing, or you can tell somebody who won't be so favorably inclined."

To my surprise, Bevvy crumbled. "All I said was that if he tried to screw around with me anymore, he'd be in even bigger trouble than he was now," she announced in a small voice, looking from Pop to me. "At least, I *think* that was all I said."

I took a moment to digest this information, then said, "Bevvy, you obviously went to a lot of trouble cutting off that bit of tape. Surely you remember *exactly* what was said."

"Those may not have been the exact words, that was the gist of it."

"If you think back carefully, maybe you can come up with the exact words," I suggested.

"What are you asking her for?" Pop asked. "Ask me."

"Ask *you?*" I turned to him, exasperated. "Pop, you weren't there. You were in Boca Raton, remember?"

"So don't ask me. Keep *phumpha-ing* around and getting nowhere."

To avoid getting into a family feud in Bevvy's presence, I summoned every drop of patience I possessed and told Pop, "All right, tell me what she said. But first, tell me why you think you know."

"For fifty years I overheard conversations at the Merkin. You think I closed my ears? Believe me, if I was the type, I could be a millionaire from the blackmail alone, not to mention the stock tips." He turned to Bevvy and asked, "You want me to say it or do you want to come clean yourself?"

"I'd rather hear your fairy tales."

Pop threw back the last of his vodka. "I believe you told Karl Krieg, 'Don't try screwing around with me again, you lousy bastard, or I'll cut your crooked heart out.' "

Bevvy turned pale.

"Do you have anything to say?" I asked her.

"About what?" Beneath that tough exterior lay a tough interior.

"The tape."

"What tape?" She stood up, picked up a letter opener from her desk and held it casually, though I sensed that she was ready to stab anyone who tried to take the tape out of her machine.

"Bevvy," I reminded her, reading her mind, "you yourself said your company logs every call, including the name and number of the caller. They find this tape missing, after you logged in many calls to and from Krieg, and the police will wonder. Once they wonder, they start digging. Once they dig, they'll find all sorts of things you've forgotten about, starting with the two Grand Jury investigations."

"My record is clean."

"I believe you, but I'm trying to find the murderer of Karl Krieg and clear all our names. And you can put down that letter opener; I'm not going to grab for that tape."

"I'll hold on to it," she said, her voice sounding slightly shrill. "Ordinary business precaution."

"Whatever makes you feel better," I spoke slowly, my mind racing to find a way to ask what I had to ask. "I need some more information from you. So I'll trade you; I'll go first, so it'll be easy to fool me if you decide that's wise. That envelope that Krieg had at the wedding? The one that the police have now? It didn't have fifty thousand dollars in it; it was full of cut-up newspaper."

Bevvy sat down and tossed the letter opener on the desk. "That's a relief; now no one can even think it was for me to bribe officials with."

"They can still think it; you know what some of my opponents have said about me in the past. Now it's your turn. When Mr. and Mrs. Krieg came in, you greeted Mrs. Krieg, but Karl said something to you, you turned red, and you didn't shake his hand. Why? What did he say?"

Bevvy gulped down her wine, then said, "I didn't shake his hand because he was a no-good slimy bastard and he wasn't welcome at Aileen's wedding. Donna, on the other hand, seemed nice and was gracious, so I welcomed her. I even took pity on her, a little, for being married to that son of—"

"That's reasonable," I cut in, "but what did he say to you, Bevvy?"

"He said, 'Forget about Monday; I got all I need from a better source.' "

This shocked me for a moment, but then, what could be expected from Karl Krieg?

"You're lucky," I said, half joking to lighten the atmosphere, "he could've not told you anything and left you waiting, all of Monday morning, in the bank's office with your lawyer. Fortunately, he's the type who gets pleasure from hurting people to their faces when they're not in a position to fight back."

"Do you think it was a pleasure to hear something like that at my daughter's wedding? I think I showed remarkable self-control in not beating his fat head in with whatever was handy."

"The problem is," I said, "the police won't believe you showed any self-control later when you stabbed him."

"Come on, Ed, do you believe I would've told you this if I were the killer?"

Pop opened his mouth to say something, but I quickly jumped in with, "I never believed you were the killer, Bevvy, and I still don't, but I have to question you like this. And all this shows is that Krieg hurt you financially, professionally, and personally, in several ways."

"Is that what you're going to tell the police?" she asked.

"I'm not going to tell the police anything—and I hope you realize how little good this does for my relations with them—until I know who the murderer is. When I know that, I'll tell the police everything I know about the murderer and nothing about the rest of the suspects."

I motioned to Pop that we were leaving. Bevvy looked as though she was ready to fall apart. I didn't want to see her like that.

Unless she was the killer, of course.

Pop and I walked in silence for a while, except when we were interrupted by someone who wanted to greet me and shake my hand.

Finally, Pop couldn't hold himself in any longer. "Who do we go after next?" he asked.

"I think it should be Ken Lang," I said. "But not right now. He's an accountant, and he'll be very busy."

"Why busy? April 15 is over. He has to be loafing right now."

"There are always the people who get their forms ready the last second." Like me, though I'd never tell Pop that. "Guaranteed he's working today. Maybe even on Sunday too."

"So what? He can't spare fifteen minutes?"

"It's not the time, Pop; it's the interruption in the flow of thought and the emotional upset. It's me, too. I have to think about the latest development with Bevvy."

"You can't think while we're working on something else? Where does he live? I'll bet it's not far from here."

"It isn't," I said, "but I don't want to talk to him today. I have other things on my mind, not just the murder—city things to think about. But I promise you, when we get back home, I'll call May Lang and try to see Ken tomorrow."

"At his office," Pop said, "not his home. Guys talk differently in front of their wives."

"Thanks for explaining it to me, Pop."

"And I can go with you?"

I hesitated. "Look, Pop, I appreciate your interest, but—"

"I'm glad, because I appreciate the opportunity to be of service. You let me know what time the appointment with Ken Lang is, and I'll be ready and waiting to join you."

I sighed. I'd have to find a couple of pinochle players for Pop; otherwise, he'd be sitting in my office in no time, "helping" me run the city.

FIFTEEN

"I know he works hard," I told May Lang Sunday morning—I hadn't been able to reach her until now—"and that the tax season isn't over till the end of June on account of lazy clients who don't even open their mail until after April 15"—like me, I didn't bother to add—"but it's very important that I see him."

"What happens if you don't see him?" she asked.

"You find a good criminal lawyer and pay him a big retainer. The police commissioner is not happy that a prominent"—May made a vomiting noise—"I know Karl Krieg was a crook and a liar and everything bad, but he was a prominent citizen and he was murdered right under the commissioner's nose. And my nose, too."

"And that's your big worry, Ed? That it was done under your nose?"

"It has repercussions. But as far as you're concerned, and as far as Ken's concerned, the police are very anxious to get the killer. And when they're this anxious, they often get the killer. I happen to know that the police are working very hard on this case."

"You know Ken's not a killer. Even you are more likely to murder someone than he is. Ken's the nicest, sweetest, most peaceful man I've ever known."

"You know that and I know that, May, but how often have you

heard on TV, 'John was such a nice, sweet, gentle boy. Who'd ever imagine he'd chop up six people?' Sweet, nice, gentle, and peaceful don't mean a thing to the police. The threat 'I'll kill him' means more than all the niceness adjectives.''

May was silent for a while, then she said, "Why do you want to talk to him a second time? You've spoken to him once and the police have done it twice. Isn't that enough?''

"No, it isn't," I said. "I've spoken to all the prime suspects once already, and I don't have the slightest idea who did it. So maybe I didn't ask the right questions, or I didn't ask them in the right way, or I didn't notice something that I heard, or I didn't understand it, or the suspects didn't answer truthfully, or *something.*''

"Or maybe you're not competent to be a detective?" May suggested.

I had to swallow hard for that one.

But of course May didn't know how I'd solved the Vinnie Lobosco case, and that was when I was a lot younger and not as smart and as experienced as I am now.

"You'd better hope I'm competent to be a detective, May," I informed her. "Three of the prime suspects are friends of mine''— for her sake, I included Ken in that count, even though I barely knew him—"and I sort of like the other two as well. I'm not saying I'd lie or conceal evidence to protect a murderer who happened to be a friend, but I'd be understanding and try to present the evidence in the best light.''

"I'll ask Ken if he'll see you again," May said, and there was a clattering sound as she put the phone down.

While I was waiting for her, Pop stuck his head into the room. He was wearing his Sunday morning uniform of pajamas, a robe, slippers, and a golf hat. In one hand, he held a mug of steaming coffee, and in the other, an enormous bundle of Sunday newspapers.

At least he'd be occupied for a while, I thought gratefully, hoping I could sneak away without him.

"Any luck?" he asked hopefully.

I shrugged and mouthed "Not yet," then waved him away.

Instead of leaving, he settled himself in a chair near the door and waited.

May came back two seconds later. "If you come right now, and limit yourself to about fifteen minutes, it'll be okay. Ken's in his office, working, but he agreed to make time for you."

"Thanks," I said. "Where is his office?"

"Right here at home. Actually it started out as a study, but you know how it is with someone as conscientious as Ken. Are you bringing Lolly with you?"

"No. I doubt she'd want to interrogate someone she likes as much as she likes you and Ken."

"But you do, Ed?"

"I don't want to either, but I must. As mayor I've had to do many things I don't enjoy. It comes with the job."

May sighed. "After you finish torturing Ken, why don't you stay and have tea and cake? I made a Sacher torte yesterday."

I had no doubt that she extended this invitation to prove a point. But I've never been one to turn down a freshly made Sacher torte.

"I promise not to torture Ken," I told her, "and I'd love to have tea and chocolate cake with you. Two slices? With whipped cream?" The heavy Viennese specialty absolutely *must* be slathered with whipped cream.

"Either you really love Sacher torte, or you're bringing someone with you."

"Both, actually."

"Not a cop, I hope," May said.

"My father, who's worse than a cop, in some ways. But the two slices are for me."

With my gang of bodyguards in their usual formation, I took Pop—who had gotten dressed and ready in one minute flat—west along Eighty-sixth Street, the wide cross street that was the center of Yorkville.

The thoroughfare emphasized the neighborhood's German beginnings every ten feet. The shops featured German books, German popular music, and German folk arts and crafts, a wide variety of cakes and pastries, and an even wider variety of sausages.

When we got to Park Avenue, we turned left toward the Lang apartment. Park is one of the most beautiful streets in the world. Not only is it twice as wide as any other street in New York, but it has a planted center mall. The Park Avenue Association, comprised of the residents of the area, plants spring flowers in the mall and tends them. Today, the tulips were in full bloom, in every color imaginable.

Much as I love my apartment in the Village, not to mention Gracie Mansion, I've often wished I had a place on Park—especially at this time of year, with everything blossoming and fragrant.

We were at the Langs' door in fifteen minutes.

May let us in. She was gracious and friendly, though I sensed that she was nervous.

After I had introduced her to my father, whom I had warned to be on his best behavior, she took us to the end of the living room near the door to Ken's office.

"Sit down for a few minutes," she said. "He's in the middle of our tax return and if he's bothered, he could lose his whole train of thought. He should be out in a few minutes."

"It's after April 15," I said, "and he's an accountant. I would have expected him to have his return in the mail a week early."

May sighed. "It's a case of the shoemaker's children going barefoot. Accountants get a rush of returns at the last minute, so their own have to wait. It's okay; Ken put in for a late filing."

Pop looked at his watch. "How much longer will he be?" he asked.

"Any minute now," she assured him.

"Doesn't he need you for some of the tax information?" Pop asked—pretty nosy of him, I thought, but May answered willingly.

"I'm lucky. Most of the women I know have to handle the bankbooks and the regular income and outgo. Ken knows everything and he does everything. I don't even have to balance the checkbooks and feel happy when my monthly bank balance is only ten dollars off like my friends do."

Just then, the office door opened and Ken stuck his head out. "Come in," he said, sounding irritated.

"I'll get the tea and cake ready," May said, then waved a warning finger at me and added, "but remember, the whipped cream disappears after fifteen minutes."

We sat on the chairs opposite Ken's cluttered desk as he closed the door.

"I'll make this quick, of course," I told Ken, "because May said you were pressed for time."

"Till the beginning of June I'll be pressed for time," Ken said, "and then I have to start worrying about the quarterly reports. It never ends."

"Let me ask you something," Pop said, starting the interrogation right away; Bernie Koch is not known for his subtlety. "You're one of the owners of a big firm, doing complicated numbers work and advising big companies about taxes and money and business. Why did your wife have to explain about that simple little oil deal with Karl Krieg?"

"I was angry about it," Ken said, "and I might not have described it accurately. May knew the deal as well as I did."

"So angry you couldn't think straight?" I jumped into the conversation before Pop could respond. "You, a strictly facts and figures guy?"

"I'd been cheated and made a fool of so, yes, I was angry."

"You hated Karl Krieg for making a fool of you," I said simply.

"I didn't hate him, I was angry about the deal."

"And ten years later you're still so angry with him, you can't talk straight?" Pop put in. "Come on, Mr. Lang, you hated him."

"So I hated him," Lang admitted. "Big deal. Everyone who knew him hated him. Even his wife."

"But ten years later?" Pop pressed on. "Three hundred thousand dollars divided by ten is thirty thousand a year. Not peanuts, but you can afford that."

"Nobody likes to be cheated," Ken said, "or be made a fool of."

"Did you make the arrangements to sue the Krieg estate the way I suggested when we last spoke?" I asked.

"No, I've been too busy lately."

"In the ten years since you were cheated, did you and the other partners ever sue Krieg?"

"I don't know what the others did."

"But you didn't sue?"

"It would hurt my company to have me look like a fool publicly. I give tax advice and opinions on deals like that. We could be out of business in one day if this got out."

"Let's try a different angle," Pop said.

Uh-oh, I thought.

"Your wife knows all about the oil deal, about all your deals. Why isn't she sitting here right now?"

Okay, so Pop was on the right track. I always give credit where it's due, so I flashed him an appreciative look.

"She doesn't like this kind of antagonistic questioning."

"Antagonistic?" Pop looked offended. "This is just looking for information, for the truth."

I looked over my shoulder to make sure May hadn't sneaked in, then said, in a low voice, "You're hiding something from her, aren't you?"

Ken's face got red. "You're crazy; May and I have no secrets from each other."

"So why are you so all shook up? Sure, you're hiding something from her. So what could it be?" I stared hard at Ken Lang. "Women? No. Drinking? No. Drugs? No. Money? No— *Yes!*" I said triumphantly, reaching the conclusion based on the look on Ken's face when I mentioned the M-word.

It was Pop's turn to pat me on the back. "Good work, Eddie."

"Money," I repeated, focusing on Ken. "Yup, that's what it's all about. So why should you hide money from your wife? You both eat out of the same pot, you both agree on where to invest your money, you both . . . That's it! You spent money on—no, wrong, she wouldn't care if you spent a thousand dollars on a tie for yourself; knowing May, she'd be happy if it made you happy."

Ken shifted in his chair and said, "This is crazy, I don't—"

"You invested money without talking to her about it," I continued, cutting him off. "Big money. Of course. It has to be that. Three hundred thousand dollars. You bought *two* shares of the Krieg oil deal without even telling her about it afterward."

"I didn't, I—"

"It's easy to trace," I said.

Suddenly, Ken buried his face in his hands. "I did it for May and the children," he said, and though his voice was muffled, I could hear it trembling. "It looked like such a good deal, an investment for the family's future, that when Krieg offered me one more share at the same price, with one minute to make my mind up, I wrote him out a check. I didn't have anything liquid left, so to cover the check, I borrowed from the partners' fund at the office—with their knowledge and approval—and I've been paying it back over the past ten years. That's how everyone knows about it. What they don't know is that I bought the two shares."

Pop waited until Ken regained control of himself and looked up at us before he said, "Okay, so he conned you out of six hundred thousand. You worked hard and it's over with now. Why didn't you put it out of your mind? Why do you have to drive yourself crazy and hurt your family? Go tell your wife; she'll forgive you. I can tell."

"Maybe if I had done it right away," Ken said, "she would've yelled at me for a couple of days, but to keep this from her for ten years . . . ? She'd never trust me again. I couldn't live with that."

"So that's why you got upset when you were questioned about the Krieg murder," I realized. "The police don't know about this last part?"

"No, and I don't want them to know. It would just make it look more like I killed him."

"Unless you're the murderer," I said, "I don't see any reason to tell this to anybody."

Ken looked relieved. "Thanks, Ed."

"A couple of last questions," I said. "At the time the chairs were being brought out, you were standing in the corner where Krieg had to pass when he was going to the back. Did you talk to him?"

"To that bastard? Never."

"So he talked to you," Pop jumped in. "What did he say?"

"No— Nothing!"

"Yes," Pop said. "It's written all over your face. Don't argue with me; I've waited some of the biggest con artists in the world, and I've got good hearing. So let's see, what was it he could've said to you that got you all upset? Good morning? Nice day? Where've you been all these years? Nah, I don't think so. Seen any good shows lately? I sincerely doubt it."

"It's obvious," I said. "Krieg somehow found out . . . You know how talk goes around: One person tells two people, each of them tells two more and each of them tells two more, and before you know it, a hundred people know. Krieg found out that your wife thought that you had bought only one share. So what he said to you in those few seconds, almost in passing, was, approximately, 'Hello sucker, you're going to send me a hundred a week or I tell your wife about the second share.' Right?"

Lang crumpled. No answer was necessary, so I went on. "A hundred a week wouldn't be so terrible financially, Ken. You could manage that and, since you handle the family accounts, May would never know. But you knew that a blackmailer is never satisfied with the come-on; the price goes up every few months until you're bled dry."

"And that's why you killed him," Pop said. "That's why you—"

"Whoa. Hang on, Pop. You're too fast. You can't jump from Krieg's trying to blackmail Ken to Ken's murdering him a few minutes later."

Pop sent me a dirty look and clamped his mouth shut.

"I didn't kill him," Ken said. "I didn't kill anybody."

I turned back to him. "You've withheld a lot of important information from the police, and a lot of important information from me. What else are you holding back?"

"Nothing, I swear." He looked ready to have a nervous breakdown. "Nothing."

"You'd better be telling the truth," I warned. "Because if I find out that you've held back anything, no matter how small, friend or not, I'll tell the police everything I know."

"I've told you everything."

"Okay," I said, letting out the breath I was holding, thankful that I couldn't prove—for the while, at least—that Ken Lang was the murderer.

His shoulders were sagging and he looked pale. I realized he needed a little time to compose himself, so I turned to my father.

"Pop? Do us a favor. Go out to Mrs. Lang and tell her that we'll be busy a few more minutes. In fact, why don't you bring the Sacher torte in here? I get two portions. And tell her that I get lots of whipped cream; she'll understand."

"I didn't want to say anything in front of Lang," Pop said when we were in the elevator on the way down to the lobby of the Langs' building, where the bodyguards were waiting, "but you had a hell of a nerve stopping me when I had him on the ropes. Another ten seconds and he would've confessed."

"In the state he was in," I said, "he would've confessed to killing Lincoln, so what good is that?"

"If he'd confessed to killing Krieg, a big load would've been taken off your shoulders. Why do you think I'm doing this?"

"Because it's more fun than pinochle and you don't like folk dancing."

"Okay, that too."

That too? That was it. I know my father.

"Pop, I was once an attorney, remember? Here's how I'd attack the case. Mr. Lang was, for most of the reception, pinned in a corner by Mrs. Laura Winter. Being a gentleman, Mr. Lang could not and did not push his way past her; he was in that corner for good. There is no way that Mr. Lang could know that Karl Krieg would push his way past him and go into the back aisle. And most important, there is no way Mr. Lang could have gotten the murder weapon into the reception in the first place."

"Aren't you forgetting something, Mr. Big Shot Defense Attorney? I still got a good memory and you told me that Mr. Lang was not being baby-sat by anybody for at least two minutes and it took only two seconds to kill Krieg."

"Maybe three, but that's not the point. How did Mr. Lang— granted he knew that Krieg was going to be there—know that Krieg was going to blackmail him?"

"Easy. Krieg called him a couple of days before and told him. We know that Krieg was the kind of guy who liked to twist the knife in his victims."

"I'll accept all of that," I said. "Now tell me how Mr. Lang got the knife into the chapel."

Pop's face fell. "I don't know that yet, but I'll figure it out."

Feeling smug, I reached out and pushed the Down button.

___ SIXTEEN

As we drove south along Second Avenue on the way to City Hall, my bodyguard whistled cheerfully in the seat beside me.

Meanwhile, I stared glumly out at the sun-splashed world, wrapped in a black mood at still having the Krieg murder hanging over my head.

Like most other people who work for a living—and if you think being mayor isn't work, you try it sometime—I hate Mondays. They're even worse when a large part of the weekend—in terms of emotional involvement—is spent in trying to see if friends of yours are murderers.

One thing I'd have to do today, no matter what, was have a good talk with Moshe Gur. In that short conversation on the phone with his wife—which was nowhere near as good as a face-to-face interrogation where I could watch the questionee's reactions—I had learned that the sweet-looking Gur was a trained, even an expert, killer. Moshe had even admitted that himself.

Knocking off Karl Krieg, right under the noses of a hundred people and three detectives, could have been child's play for him. In fact, given the circumstances at the wedding, he could have done it a lot more quickly and conveniently than any of the other suspects.

"Are you taking part in that big Earth Day rally this week, Mr.

Mayor?" the bodyguard, whose name was Connor, broke off his whistling to ask.

"You bet," I said, dragging my thoughts away from the murder. "Any rally, parade, or festival happens in this city, and you can be sure that I'll be there if I possibly can." I gestured at the radio, which he had turned down low, just as Charley always did. "So, what's doing? Anything I should know about?"

"Nah, not much. The D train isn't running, and there's a big jam-up in the Lincoln Tunnel because of a stalled bus, but that's about as exciting as the news gets today."

"That's what I like to hear." I settled back against the seat.

Today the limo I was riding in was being used as the lead car, with the regular lead car trailing us; another of the security team's many little tricks to confuse possible terrorists as to where the mayor was.

As we drove, I was looking around the way I usually do, checking the state of the city.

We stopped for a light, and I examined the people waiting in line at an ATM machine on the corner. They all looked so unruffled, so wrapped up in their own little worlds, hiding behind their sunglasses and their Walkmans and their newspapers.

I envied them. *They* didn't have to worry about running the city or solving murder cases.

Well, with any luck, it wouldn't be long before I figured out who had murdered Krieg. Then I could go back to concentrating on being mayor . . . and figuring out how to convince my parents to start their visit with Sophie in Scarsdale a few days early.

I called Lolly as soon as I got to the office.

"I'm going to interrogate Moshe Gur this afternoon, late. If you'd like to be there, when are you free?"

"Will that be in City Hall?" she asked. "Or someplace else?"

"I think City Hall would be best, in terms of privacy. And we'll need it so that we can talk the way we have to talk now."

"It'll be that rough, Ed?"

"I hope so," I said. "We're at the stage now—it's been over a week since Krieg was killed—where if we don't solve this soon, we'll never solve it. The police don't seem to be making much progress, so it's up to us, as far as I'm concerned. And if we have to be brutal, then . . ." I trailed off with a shrug.

There was a moment of silence, and then Lolly said, "I've been talking to Bevvy, and to May Lang, too. Did you have to be so rough on them?"

"Yes, and I'm glad I was. I turned up some new information that your sweet innocent friends had been keeping from me. Do you want to hear what it is?"

"Absolutely not," she said. "I don't care if Bevvy's been sleeping with the whole cast of *La Cage Aux Folles* and has been drinking a liter of Grand Marnier a day, she's my friend and I love her and she didn't kill that no-good bastard who deserved to be killed."

"And if it turns out to be Ken Lang?" I asked.

"Slightly better. Maybe one percent slightly better, but that's all."

"I'm glad you're so open-minded. That's why it was better you didn't come along for those two interrogations."

"Bevvy said you brought your father. She wasn't as charmed by him as I always have been."

"Well, that stands to reason. In addition to the comics, a lot of crooks, con men, and grifters must have eaten at the Merkin Deli, too. I think that's where he learned his questioning technique. I did my best to keep him quiet, but you know how that goes. So anyway, when will you come here to grill Moshe Gur?"

"Three o'clock, but I have to leave no later than four. I'm meeting my trainer at the gym. You miss one day's workout, and a ton of cellulite grows on your thighs that very night. Your office?"

"It's the least private place in City Hall—people walk in and out like it's Grand Central Station—but if I station Rosemary at the door, we'll manage."

After I hung up, I checked my watch. My first meeting of the morning promised to be an interesting one. It was with Kevin Wagner, the famous, flamboyant television producer. He was in town from LA this week to unveil his new fall series for the advertising and media executives at the annual Upfront presentations.

The show, "Midtown," was a crime drama set in New York, and was supposedly going to be pretty controversial. Wagner wanted to talk to me about getting permission to film some additional scenes on location. Not only that, but Rosemary had said that he was supposedly planning to invite me to make a guest appearance, playing myself, on an episode.

Since Wagner wasn't supposed to show up for another ten minutes, I settled myself in my comfortable leather chair and reached for my briefcase.

I pulled out the envelope of wedding photos that Don O'Sullivan had given me. I'd studied them countless times over the weekend, but I couldn't help feeling like I kept missing something.

Hoping I'd catch whatever I'd missed, I started going through them again.

Lolly came into my office at a quarter to three that afternoon. I had warned her that Moshe Gur is always early.

"I had to rush to make it here on time. I hope you appreciate the effort I'm making for you," she said, plopping herself down into a chair.

"You know I appreciate it."

"I'm not looking forward to this. Especially after how Bevvy went on and on, telling me how you and your father gave her a very hard time on Saturday."

"Not as hard a time," I pointed out, "as the DA would have given her on the stand had she been arrested for murder."

"I told you that she didn't do it."

"Would you please put that in writing so I can use it to convince the DA not to put her in jail? Come on, Lolly, I'm looking for firm evidence and you're giving me feelings."

"My feelings are never wrong in important things. You think my company was anywhere near half as big as it is now when my Joe—when I inherited it?"

Joe had been her husband, and Lolly can never bring herself to refer directly to his death.

"Listen," I told her, "I'm not saying you're not great at everything you do; all I want is something I can give the police. And I do respect your feelings. Wasn't I the one who asked you to work with me in this case?"

"And weren't you the one who got two of my friends mad at

me? What else are you going to do to get more people to hate me?"

"The next one's no problem," I said. "Moshe Gur."

"I know, but he bothers me," Lolly said. "I hate being around saints."

"Moshe? He's not a saint—nowhere near—he's just Orthodox. And I'm not going to go easy on him today. He's a lot tougher than he looks; used to be a commando in the Israeli Army. Besides, I hit on another good idea that may have some bearing on what we get from Moshe."

"What is it?"

"You'll see. Anyway, we have one advantage; he always tells the exact, literal truth. I won't call it a weakness on his part; he's so bright he can answer your question truthfully, and still conceal the information he doesn't want you to have."

Just then Rosemary buzzed. "Commissioner Gur is here."

"Send him in," I said, motioning Lolly to sit where she could watch him but where he'd have trouble seeing her.

Gur came in and I instantly saw that he looked very unhappy.

"I haven't heard of any problems in my department," he said, "and Mrs. Winter is sitting in, so this has to be about the Krieg murder."

"Sit down, Moshe," I invited.

He sat, moving his chair so that he could see me and Lolly at the same time. Gur is the most intelligent commissioner I have . . . you can't pull anything over on him, which I would normally consider a good thing.

"Yes, it is about the Krieg murder," I admitted. "I want to ask you some questions."

"You've already asked me and my wife all the necessary questions, Ed."

"Not all the necessary questions, just the questions I knew I should ask at the time. Based on what I've found out from the other prime suspects the second time around, I know more questions to ask that will help throw light on the problems. I hope you'll cooperate."

"Of course I'll cooperate," he said shortly. "I have no reason not to."

"Good," I said. "I was thinking a little while ago, putting together in my mind all the statements made by our prime suspects, and I realized there was a time when where you were was not noticed by anyone I questioned. This was shortly before the chairs were pulled out and everyone sat down and I went to the lectern to perform the wedding ceremony. Where were you?"

"It's hard to be exact. Somewhere in the middle of the crowd on the right side of the room as you face front."

"Wasn't Karl Krieg there at about that time?"

"I saw him several times in that general area."

"At that time?"

"When I was in that area."

"Did you speak to him at about that time?" I felt like a prosecuting attorney trying to drag a vital reponse from an unfriendly witness.

"I have never spoken to Mr. Krieg."

"Did he speak to you?"

Moshe thought for a long time, but there was no way out, so he folded. "Yes."

"Tell me everything he said to you."

Moshe hesitated, then told me, "He said, 'I can get this planted where they'll think it's yours, so you better be nice.' "

"Was 'this' an envelope he had in the breast pocket of his jacket—one that looked like it had a lot of money in it?"

"Yes." Moshe's face was darker than usual.

"Is there any way you could have stopped him from getting it planted?"

"No."

"If found, the envelope would have destroyed you professionally and personally. Possibly have sent you to jail?"

"I might even have been shunned by my community, and my children might have lost faith in me."

"Would you have—shall we say—cooperated with him to prevent this tragedy?"

"No. If he won the project, I intended to resign."

I frowned. "Did you intend to tell me about this when you resigned?"

"No, the shame of having an evil person like that think he could blackmail me into helping him steal and cheat . . . I didn't want you to think I could be forced to do wrong."

"You realize this gives you a very strong motive to kill Krieg?"

"I did *not* murder Karl Krieg!"

I looked at him. "You knew you would tell me this before you walked in, didn't you."

"I knew you were smart enough to ask the right questions in the right way." He got up. "I want to leave now. So tell me one thing: Are you going to tell this to the police?"

"Only if you're the murderer."

He left, moving fast and closing the door behind him with a resolute click.

I swung my chair toward Lolly. "The last time I talked to him, he differentiated between killing and murder. Murder is against the Ten Commandments, but there are many reasons a man can kill."

"Then why did you accept his answer? Why not ask the right question in the right way?"

"Because I don't believe he's the murderer and I don't want to embarrass him by asking that question. I still have to work with him."

So I'm human, too: Lolly with Bevvy and the Langs, and me with Moshe Gur.

Before Lolly could point that out, I asked her, "Did you see anything in his face to show he wasn't being truthful about anything?"

"A lot of pain, that's all. No lies."

"What about tomorrow?" I asked. "Want to come with me to visit the Mardins?"

"Where are they?"

"Brooklyn, in an industrial neighborhood not far from the Queens border. I want to question them in their native habitat."

"You'll pick me up?"

"With pleasure. And take you home."

"You know something, Ed?" she said. "Playing detective isn't all fun. Somebody's going to suffer. And it'll be a nice somebody;

all our prime suspects are good people and the victim was a bastard."

"That's how life sometimes works, Lolly, and there's nothing we can do about it."

SEVENTEEN

On Tuesday, with Lolly at my side in the limo, we drove across the Brooklyn Bridge, past Flatbush Avenue, and onto the Brooklyn-Queens Expressway. I knew when we reached the right neighborhood—there were acres and acres of industrial buildings.

Jomar Development Corporation was housed in a high metal-clad building with a big yard, surrounded by a chain-link fence, where a large number of heavy construction machines of all kinds were stored. Lolly and I got out of the limo and walked to what looked like the front door.

We made a natural mistake and entered the building—the door wasn't locked—through the garage and shop, where about ten men dressed in work clothes were cleaning the engines of trucks and bulldozers.

When he saw us, one of the men pointed to a door on the short side of the garage and shouted something. It was muffled by the noise of the shop, but it wasn't hard to figure out what he meant and we went through the side door.

Beyond it was a long hallway. All the offices that lined it were empty, doors open, but no names or titles on the wall.

Lolly and I moved along until we came to the end office.

This was clearly Joan and Frank Mardin's office. I knocked on the closed door.

"Come in," Joan's voice called.

The first thing I saw was that Joan, in a black business suit, was sitting behind her desk working on her computer, with Frank sitting alongside her in stained work clothes. The screen was tilted so that it was visible from the doorway, and when we stepped into the room, Joan saved what looked to me like a spreadsheet. She shut off the computer, and invited us to sit down on the chairs across the desk from her.

After we had all shaken hands, Joan asked, "Would you like a drink?"

"Do you have any Diet Coke?" I asked.

"As a matter of fact, I think we do. Mrs. Winter?"

"I'll have one, too."

Frank reached over behind him, got four small cans of soda, passed two to me, and opened the other two for himself and Joan.

"As I told you on the phone," I said, "I'm going through a second round of talks with all the prime suspects, of which you are one." I nodded to Frank.

He didn't look happy. Could you blame him?

"I'm doing this," I went on, "because, in my first round, I picked up some information that showed me I hadn't asked the right questions in the right way. I also want to thank you in advance for your cooperation. Now, do you have anything to tell me that you might have forgotten about the first time?"

"What do you mean when you say I'm one of the 'prime suspects'?" Frank asked. "The first time, in the restaurant, you didn't say I was a 'prime suspect.' What you said was that you wanted information."

"You're right," I said. "I wasn't trying to keep things from you; I just forgot. But to put your mind at ease, what we call prime suspects are any people who were in or near the back of the room, on the right side of the room as you faced forward, between the time the chairs were taken out of the alcoves and the time the wedding ceremony started."

"That wasn't a very long time," Joan said. "It couldn't have been more than two or three minutes. How about adding in the time that was taken up when everyone started to leave? After the toasts were drunk?"

"That's theoretically possible, but it's very unlikely. With everybody crowded in the back aisle, where the body was found, it would've been practically impossible for someone not to notice Karl Krieg either standing still or going in the opposite direction. And if he were doing that, why would he? Stand still, I mean, or move against the current."

"I can't think why," Joan said. "And as I play it over in my mind, I don't remember seeing anyone other than the ones I told you about—the prime suspects? Nobody, including the prime suspects, seemed to be acting suspiciously in any way. At least, not that I noticed."

"Me neither," Frank said. "Everybody was acting normal."

"That's the answer I got from everybody," I said. "If it weren't for the body that I saw with my own eyes, I'd wonder if there was a murder to begin with. Maybe I need a different approach."

"The knife?" Joan reminded me. "Have you figured out yet how it could have been brought in?"

"No," I said. "I'm working on the idea that when I find the killer, then I'll know how he got the knife into the chapel."

I didn't tell her about the elusive *something* that kept flitting around the edges of my mind. Something I felt that I should be remembering.

"But you haven't found the killer yet, have you?" Joan asked. "Are we the last ones to be questioned on the second round?"

"One more, Mrs. Mardin, and that will be tomorrow afternoon. Then I'll spend the weekend thinking and everything will fall into place."

"Frank is an engineer," Joan said. "One of the best." She turned to her husband. "Is there any way to get a knife into the chapel?"

He shook his head glumly. "As far as I know, from what I've read about the case, it would have to be impossible. Now, if you'll excuse me, I have to get back—"

"I have another question," I cut in. "I noticed when we met for lunch that you, Joan, were wearing a simple, neat, business outfit but Frank was wearing oil-stained denims. Today it's the same thing. Frank was working some of the day in the repair shop."

"We all do what we have to do," Frank said with a shrug.

"You also said that you had worked on getting ready to bid the Muni Yard Project from the day it was announced, checking all parts of the bid process, using your own architects and engineers for months until you knew it was a doable job."

"That's the way we work," Joan said.

"Your offices are empty and the few men you have left are all doing machinery repair and maintenance work. What I read from that is that you've laid off all your people except for a few key men and you're keeping them busy doing odds and ends, nothing productive."

I paused, waiting for one of them to comment, but they were silent, as if waiting for me to go on. So I did.

"You have a lot of equipment in the yard and in the shop, all clean and oiled and shiny, which means that you haven't rented it to other contractors. So it's obvious that you hadn't bid for any work—putting all your chips on the Muni Yard Project—and hadn't taken any work for months so that you'd be prepared for the project when you won it."

"That's the nature of this business," Joan said, with a glance at Frank, who nodded. "All chicken or all feathers."

"There's more to it than that," Lolly put in. "You were counting on Beverly Benson to do your filings and get your approvals and permits and by the time you found out that she was working with Karl Krieg, you had neither the time nor the ability to complete the paperwork required to even be considered for the project. In addition, the mortgage payments on all the additional machinery you bought will soon come due."

"In other words," I concluded, "in three months or less, you're dead broke and out of business."

There was a moment of silence, during which Lolly sipped her soda, I tapped my fingers patiently on the arm of my chair, and the Mardins kept their faces carefully neutral.

"We've been in worse fixes in our life," Joan said at last. "We never gave up and we won't give up now. If it weren't for Krieg's death, I would've sat down with Beverly Benson—we've worked with her before and she knows how good we are—on the Monday after the wedding, and told her to dump Krieg."

"Why?" Lolly asked.

"Not just because he's a liar and a crook, but because she'd never see a penny of the money he owes her, and I'll bet he hasn't paid her a penny to date. I would've offered Beverly the same as he promised to pay her, from the first set of requisitions, in writing, and I think she would've taken it. Once we were designated as developer of the site, the banks would've been chasing us, waving money at us, and we'd be all right again."

"You're gamblers," Lolly said, "betting your whole life on a single card."

"That's the building business in New York City," Frank said, "and I love it."

I turned back to Joan. "Do you realize that you've just told me that you have a terrific motive for killing Krieg?"

"Wrong," Joan said, shaking her head firmly. "Why should we take the trouble? Why should we risk getting caught and going to jail? What I told you was what we were going to do on Monday, after the wedding. You want to do something useful? Check and see if Krieg paid Benson more than a tiny fraction of what he owes her, if that much. If I'm wrong, I'll confess to the murder in front of witnesses. And while you're at it, ask her—you don't even have to tell me the answer—if she would've taken my proposition on Monday if Krieg were still alive. I want to hear you say it."

I looked to Lolly. She thought for a moment, then said, "As a businesswoman, I can confidently say that Bevvy Benson would have accepted Joan Mardin's arrangement even if Krieg were still alive."

Joan looked at Lolly sharply. "You're her closest friend, aren't you? Beverly Benson's I mean?"

"We're friends," Lolly said carefully, "but not associated in business in any way."

" 'Not associated' instead of 'I don't know.' " Joan smiled. "I'm calling Bevvy first thing Monday morning. And I really wouldn't mind if you tell her everything I said."

As we left, I said, "I knew you were good in business, Lolly, but I didn't know how good. Thanks. This may be the break I was looking for."

_____ EIGHTEEN

It was raining like crazy on Wednesday morning, the kind of dark, violent storm that makes 7:00 A.M. look like the middle of the night.

As we headed downtown in the limo via Second Avenue, I checked to see how the city was holding up in the nasty weather. Almost all of the drains appeared to be working perfectly and the only problem I could see was the idiot drivers who believed their tires' ability to grip the pavement wasn't affected by the water and so drove in wet weather exactly the way they drove under dry conditions. Which was badly, since dopes are dopes in all kinds of weather.

What the city needed, I mused as I watched a beat-up yellow cab come within a fraction of an inch of the back of a Ford Explorer carrying a family of five, was a bunch of heavy armored cars on the lookout for dangerous drivers. When an armored car saw a likely suspect in the rearview mirror, it would immediately pull in front of that driver and slam on the brakes. The bad driver's car would slam into the back of the armored car and a cop would get out and give a ticket to the tailgater. I'd even put Vinnie Lobosco in charge of the system, as commissioner of Rear Ends.

What a lovely fantasy. Too bad I had the usual headaches waiting for me at City Hall as well as a bunch of reporters in the Press Room, wanting to hear about how the city was going to handle

Smokey Blaze's lawsuit. The notorious stripping fireman had been all over tabloid television last night, telling his side of the story. I wasn't looking forward to dealing with a sensational scandal first thing on this gloomy morning, but I didn't exactly have a choice.

Hanging over everything like Al Capp's Joe Bftsplk's cloud, was the murder of Karl Krieg. I kept going over and over everything I'd heard from the prime suspects, all five of them. I couldn't seem to overcome the nagging feeling that I was overlooking something important.

I'd interrogated them all twice—except for Donna Krieg, but if Lolly was free, we'd take care of Donna today—and come up with nothing. Well, not exactly nothing.

For one thing, they were all liars, just as my father had suspected. Or, to be accurate, none of them gave us all the information we needed. Every single suspect had deliberately *withheld* the full information. Now I didn't doubt that some of them were still sitting on information that was critical to the case. Maybe not in itself—that would be too much to hope for—but stuff that, when put together, would tell me clearly and unequivocally who the killer was.

And that was another problem. All the prime suspects, as far as I could tell, were good guys, and I didn't want to see any of them caught and dragged off in chains. Or handcuffs, leg irons, whatever—none of the above exactly created a pleasant image.

What I really wanted was to find that Karl Krieg had brought the knife into the chapel himself—how, I don't know yet—intending to kill someone else, and fell on it by accident in such a way that it stabbed him exactly in the heart and, as he continued falling, the knife wiggled around, back and forth, making the cuts the coroner found.

But what about the paper napkins around the handle?

I'd have to work on that fantasy a little more.

When I got back to my office after the Smokey Blaze press conference—which, incidentally, went surprisingly well, thanks to some well-timed zingers I threw at the reporters in true Koch fashion—I called Lolly.

"I've been waiting for you to get in touch. How'd the press conference go?"

"Better than I expected."

"Good, because I heard that there's going to be an in-depth interview with good old Smokey on 'Good Afternoon, Manhattan,' today," Lolly informed me. "He's supposed to do part of his act on camera—minus the official uniform, of course."

"Of course." I checked my watch and saw that I had about two seconds before my meeting with two of the city lawyers. "Listen, Lolly," I said hurriedly, changing the subject, "I'm having Rosemary set up a meeting with Donna Krieg this afternoon at one-thirty. Do you want to come, or what?"

"Are you kidding? Not only do I want to come, but I've had a brainstorm."

"What about?"

"Donna Krieg."

"What kind of brainstorm?"

"Tell you later. And if I'm right, and if this is the big break you've been waiting for, you're going to owe me one big favor."

Intrigued, I wanted to press her for more details. Unfortunately, I was already late for my meeting, so I reluctantly said good-bye and wondered what was up Lolly's sleeve.

After a lunch of Chinese takeout that I hastily gobbled at my desk, I got my paperwork in order, then headed out for the meeting with Donna Krieg. This morning's torrential downpour had magically transformed into blue skies and warm sunshine, so I left my trench coat and umbrella at the office.

In the limo, I leaned back and tried to get my thoughts in order. It wasn't easy, since we were surrounded by honking traffic, and my backseat bodyguard, Ben Krim, was in a chatty mood.

Lolly was waiting in the lobby of her building, which was a little unusual. She scrambled into the seat beside me and the first words out of her mouth were, "We have to make a stop before we go to Donna's."

"Why? We're running late as it is," I told her, "and there was a watermain break about twenty minutes ago on East Fiftieth Street. Midtown traffic is a mess."

"Trust me. This is very, very important," she informed me, wearing a cryptic expression. She leaned forward and spoke to the driver. "Can you pull up in front of the Gristede's on the next block?"

He glanced over his shoulder at me, and I nodded. "No problem," he said, and signaled so that he could maneuver the limo across all five lanes of the jammed avenue.

As soon as we pulled up in front of the supermarket, Lolly hopped out with a chipper "Be right back."

For a change, she was true to her word. No less than five minutes passed before she bounded back to the car clutching a medium-size paper bag.

"So what's in it?" I asked as we merged back into the crawling traffic.

"Groceries," Lolly said simply.

I know she's not crazy, but there are times I can't follow her reasoning. Or any woman's, including my mother's.

"Groceries," I repeated. "Like what?"

"A baguette," she said, "cut in half so it could fit into the bag. Also a dozen eggs, a quart of milk, a tub of whipped butter, a package of stick butter, kosher salt, cracked white pepper, and a chunk of Gruyère cheese."

Now I saw what she was doing, but I didn't see how it could possibly bring us any closer to solving the case. "You're going to make a Gruyère omelette for each of us because you're afraid Donna Krieg is going to starve to death?"

"No."

I frowned. *"No?"*

"No."

"Then what?"

"I'm being mysterious, so shut up."

I shut up.

The Krieg apartment was as tastefully and expensively furnished as I had assumed it would be after I had seen how nicely Donna had been dressed at that great French restaurant Lolly took us to. The furniture was sensible modern and looked comfortable, the rugs and drapes were perfectly compatible with the walls and parquet floors, and the lamps gave a soft, warm glow that was bright enough to allow reading but did not glare.

Donna herself was in a simple hunter green sleeveless dress, slightly shorter than the one she had worn to the restaurant, and she still looked lovely.

"Come in and make yourselves at home," she said graciously, ushering us through the rooms.

"This is for you," Lolly said, holding up the grocery bag.

Donna looked a bit surprised, then said, "That's sweet of you, Mrs. Winter, but you really don't have to bring me food; I can manage a little longer with what I have."

"The praise for my charity isn't deserved, Donna," Lolly said. "All this is for our lunch. Yours too; you must be sick and tired of dry cereal, and Ed and I haven't had a bite to eat since early morning." She gave me a look that said I had better eat and not ask too many questions. "So we'll talk around the table. Where's the kitchen?"

Donna led the way. Lolly put the bag on the counter near the stove, sat at the table, and signaled me to sit down.

Before Donna could sit down too, Lolly said, "I was in the mood for a Gruyère omelette."

"Sounds delicious," Donna said, looking a little wary, I thought.

"You know," Lolly went on, sounding completely casual, though I had been forewarned that she was up to something, "I've been working since early this morning, and I'm famished. I'd love to taste your home cooking, the real good stuff." She looked at me. "You're in the mood for a homemade Gruyère omelette too, aren't you, Ed?"

I did my duty like a real man and said, meekly, "Oh, sure. I wish you knew how to make one."

"Might as well make three, Donna, right?" Lolly said, and settled back in her chair.

"Why not? It's been awhile since I've had the opportunity to cook something." Donna shrugged and walked over to the counter.

Was it my imagination, or was she a little hesitant?

I glanced at Lolly, who arched an eyebrow and tilted her head slightly in Donna's direction.

Donna was taking all the ingredients out of the bag and spread them out on the tabletop next to the big professional six-burner range. Lolly and I kept her involved in small talk while she worked, with Lolly taking the lead, since I had no idea what we were up to.

It took Donna a full minute to find a frying pan.

She had to open several drawers and doors before she found a spatula, a fork, a knife, and a bowl.

She put the frying pan on the nearest burner and, after a quick look at the knobs, turned on the right burner.

She reached for the first egg and tapped it gingerly against the edge of the bowl on the counter. When it broke, she dumped the contents, then fished inside the bowl with a flawlessly polished, raspberry-colored nail for an elusive bit of shell.

She had painstakingly cracked nine more eggs into the bowl on the counter when Lolly interrupted herself—she'd been in the middle of a description of what Mrs. Someone-or-other had worn in the Easter Parade a few weeks ago—to yell, "Stop!"

Donna jumped—and so did I—and moved quickly away from the counter.

"Stop what?" she asked, her voice slightly shrill. "What's wrong?"

"I knew you were a liar," Lolly said.

"What are you talking about?"

Lolly looked at me.

I nodded, the whole scenario having become totally clear in an instant.

Lolly pointed at Donna. "I said, you're a liar. I wanted to confirm it and I wanted Ed to see it for himself."

"What are you talking about?" Donna looked hurt.

"You were never a cook, and the tiny bit you know about making an omelette had to have come from accidentally seeing someone else cook."

"Now wait just a minute," Donna said angrily. "Where I cooked, nobody even knew how to spell Gruyère omelette, so how could you expect me to—"

"It's a waste of time trying to con me, Donna," Lolly said. "Better men than you have tried, and it cost them plenty."

"Ed, what's she trying to do to me?" Donna asked, her voice suddenly taking on a little-girl-lost wail.

It was a good act, but I wasn't going to fall for it. "Try this to begin with," I told her. "You don't seem to know where a damn thing is in your own kitchen; I'm surprised you even knew where the kitchen was."

"That's right." Lolly nodded. "A cook would've put the baguette in the oven to warm first, would've opened the tub of whipped butter as well as the stick butter to soften a little and would have opened the milk to add to the beaten eggs. She would've heated a large crepe pan—not the high-sided frying pan you picked out—to let the butter melt quickly so the beaten eggs would still be frothy when you put them into the pan. And, of course, she wouldn't have taken out a spatula and a sharp knife. If you don't like to break a baguette, you should use a serrated knife."

Lolly looked to me for backup. Since I'm no cook, I merely nodded and said to Donna, "So, to repeat, you were never a cook."

"We never did fancy French cooking in Nelson," Donna said stubbornly.

She needn't have bothered; Lolly was on a roll.

"The way you opened the eggs," she said, "was the last nail in the coffin. Anyone who's ever cooked in a place where people have to eat in a hurry doesn't use two hands to crack open an egg. Go to any hash house and watch. The cook opens the egg with one hand, spreads the shell halves with the same hand, and then throws the empty shells into the garbage pail, all in one smooth motion, and she can do it with either hand. Some good ones can even do it with two hands simultaneously."

"This isn't a hash house, and we're not in a hurry," Donna protested.

"So? You couldn't do one egg quickly now even though I've told you how to do it. I won't even bring up knowing how to roll an omelette with one hand by flipping the crepe pan or how to slide it gracefully onto the prewarmed plate."

"Big deal," Donna said. "All people exaggerate their skills. Some women"—she stared hard at Lolly's bosom, big mistake—"even wear falsies or hairpieces. What's the harm?"

"My experience has been," Lolly said succinctly, "that a person who lies—not exaggerates, *lies*—about one thing, lies about most things."

Donna raised her chin and appeared to be in full control of herself again. She was, I noted, a remarkable woman. But, of course, my money was on Lolly.

"I don't have to be insulted in my own house," Donna announced. "I thought you wanted my help, and I was willing to give it to you, but after the way you've acted, I want you to leave."

"Another mistake, Donna. Of course we'll leave." Lolly turned to me. "Get out your portable phone, Ed, and call Sergeant Deacon. Tell him we're leaving and that we know there's some important evidence in this apartment, but he'll have to tear it apart to find it. When he's done, we'll tell him where to look to find out Donna Krieg's real background to get the motive for the murder of her husband."

As I was taking the cellular phone from my breast pocket, Donna stopped me, planting a manicured hand on my sleeve. "Maybe we should talk," she said.

"Maybe *you* should talk," I told her firmly, and she nodded.

Donna led us into the living room and we sat down. "Before you start," Lolly said, "I want to straighten out a few things. First, how much older are you than everyone thinks? And this goes for what your husband thought, too."

"Four years."

"At least six. My company has people who can find out the name of your first grade teacher in two hours."

"Seven, and you can check it."

"I will."

"Feel like telling me your real name?" I asked.

"No way," Donna said. "Have your genius private eyes dig for it; they'll never find it."

"They will," I assured her. "Next, when did your mother die?"

"When I was eighteen. She was drunk, and hit a bridge abutment."

"You never had a brother, right? Remember, I check and find you've been lying, I throw you to the wolves with everything I've got on you or can get."

Donna sighed wearily. "No brothers, no sister, no nothing. I was completely on my own right after I graduated high school."

"And then you went to beauty culture school?"

"For six months. Then I became a showgirl."

"Were you ever in jail?"

"None of your damn business."

"Lolly," I said calmly, handing her my phone, "why don't you do the honors and call Sergeant Deacon? Tell him that Mrs. Krieg has a criminal record and when he takes her prints, have him check around the country for a match."

"Wait," Donna said, and Lolly stopped with her hand poised over the telephone buttons.

Donna cleared her throat, then said, "I was arrested only twice, for very minor stuff. Once for soliciting—which was a frame because I wouldn't put out for the big shot crooked cop—and once for having two joints on me. Two times. I swear."

I shrugged. "How will you live without money until your lawyer finds where your deceased husband's money is?"

"Sell off the jewelry and whatever else I have to—"

"Why do you keep lying to us?" Lolly cut in impatiently. "Do you think we're fools?"

"No, I—"

It was my turn to interrupt. "Yes, you do. Let me give you one simple example. At lunch, you said you sent money to your mother and to your brother. The mother who died when you were eighteen and the brother you never had. Let's assume Karl gave you— it must've been chicken feed for him—a check for three hundred a week to send to your mother and two hundred a week to send to your brother."

I waited for a reaction. Donna's face was a carefully detached mask, but I could sense how tense she was. After a moment of silence, I went on.

"You endorsed these checks yourself and had them placed in a money market fund through a bank in Nelson. Who was to know that it was your account? Five hundred a week with no withdrawals and no taxes, for fourteen years at, say, eight percent compounded"—I thought for a moment—"would add up to about seven hundred thousand. You could live for a while on that."

"That's my money." Donna yelled. "I earned it."

"If there are any other heirs, I doubt you'd keep a penny of it. And if the State decides it owns the money, you could end up owing the government. And this money doesn't include the petty chiseling from the odds and ends of expense money Karl gave you or the cash you got back from clothes you returned. Over fourteen years, that could add up nicely, too."

"When you buy on credit cards you can't get cash back," Donna protested, her voice rising shrilly.

"You can, when you make a deal with a store that's as crooked as you are," Lolly pointed out.

"Now that we know who you are and what you are," I said, "it's time for you to start talking. And, please, don't make trouble for yourself by lying or omitting some of the good stuff."

"And what happens after I tell you what you think you want me to?"

"If you killed your husband, I tell the police, though they really don't need me to. If you're arrested, they'll search the records all over and come up with everything that I did. If you're innocent, I keep my mouth shut. So you see, you have everything to gain by being open and honest with me and everything to lose by pissing me off." I smiled sweetly.

Donna gulped and began talking.

"Karl knew exactly who and what I was when we got married. Although I knew it wouldn't be a hell of a good marriage—it was really a business arrangement, seventy-five percent for him, twenty-five for me—it was worse than I thought it would be."

"How so?" Lolly asked.

"I never saw one penny of what he grabbed; he kept every penny hidden away someplace. But for him, the marriage gave him greater stability in the eyes of the suckers. He didn't have to worry about, for each deal, tying up with some crooked little bitch who could queer a deal either by saying the wrong thing at the wrong time, forgetting what she was supposed to be or to do, or trying to chisel an extra few bucks for herself when he was shooting for big money."

I nodded.

Lolly did too; she was still holding the phone, ready to dial at my first command.

"Then too," Donna went on, "I'm still very beautiful, even at my age, and I'm likely to stay this good for years to come. Same type as you are"—she nodded at Lolly—"and it helps take the men's eyes, and ten percent of their minds, off the fine print even if I'm just sitting around."

I chose not to comment on her looks. "How much money did Karl have stashed away?" I asked instead.

"An absolute minimum of twenty million. I figured it out from his bragging. Probably twice as much or even a little more. And I know I'm the only heir."

"And he left no notes, no clues?"

"He never put anything in writing where I could find it. A few scribbles on scraps of paper, that's all."

"You'll let us know if you find the money?"

"Of course," Donna said, making her green eyes big and round and sincere.

Big deal. I knew she was lying again.

"One last question," I said abruptly. "Where did you learn to act so smooth and personable and ladylike?"

"Showgirls have a lot of time to read," she said, "and after I was married, what with his running around with bimbos on my money, I had nothing to do all night long but read. You can learn an awful lot just from reading."

"That, you can," I agreed, looking into Donna's big eyes and almost feeling sorry for her.

Downstairs in the lobby, before we went to the limo, I said in a low voice to Lolly, "Let's get together tomorrow night and go over what we learned. We have as much information as we're ever going to get from the prime suspects, so now's the time to do it."

"Who's going to be there?" Lolly asked, casting a wary glance at the bodyguards, who hovered nearby. "Your father?"

"And my mother. She gets brilliant flashes sometimes, out of nowhere."

"What time?"

"For supper. Say seven-thirty."

"I'll be there."

"One question. Why did you start beating up on Donna right away?"

"To break her nerve. That's how women do it; maybe you should learn how to do it, too. Nah, you're glandularly deprived; it'd never work. You stick to your way and I'll stick to my way. Anyway, I knew she was a liar. A cook in a diner at the age of twelve? And marrying Karl Krieg for love? She must've read a lot of bodice rippers."

"I almost believed her when she said it the first time."

"Just make sure to take me along," Lolly said, "when you viciously interrogate anyone over twelve wearing a size twenty-eight bra, A-cup."

NINETEEN

The four of us, Pop, Mom, Lolly, and I, were seated at the big rectangular walnut dining table in Gracie Mansion, sipping decaffeinated tea and noshing on the triple layer chocolate cake my mother had made that very afternoon.

I shudder to think of what my chef, Lucien, must have gone through when Lillian Koch marched into his kitchen and insisted on taking over. Lucien is somewhat—shall we say—territorial. And my mother is even more so. I'm glad I wasn't around to witness the coup d'état. My only role had been to give my shaken chef the weekend off to recover from the ordeal.

We had all agreed not to discuss the case until we had finished our dessert. It would have been bad for the digestion, as my mother put it.

"The trick to making a good, moist chocolate cake," my mother was saying to Lolly as I pushed my plate away, "lies in my secret ingredient."

"What is it, Mrs. Koch?" Lolly asked, scraping the last few crumbs from the simple blue-and-white china plate with her fork.

"You'll never guess." My mother nudged her arm. "But go ahead. Try."

Pop rolled his eyes. "Not this again."

I'd been through this before, too—every single time Mom made her cake for someone who had never tasted it before. But I needed a few more minutes to collect my thoughts before we started discussing the Krieg case anyway, so I didn't protest.

"Um . . . sour cream?" Lolly ventured.

"Nope."

I leaned back in my chair, closed my eyes, and struggled to catch the elusive thought that kept evading my consciousness.

There was something I was missing . . . something big. Something obvious.

If I could just . . .

"Pudding?"

"Nope."

"Cream cheese?"

"Uh-uh."

"I give up."

"Don't give up," Mom said. "Go ahead . . . give it another try."

So Lolly did.

And I kept thinking.

And Pop sat there, tapping his fingers on the table until he obviously couldn't take it any longer.

Finally, he burst out, "What is this, a recipe party? The ingredient is tomato soup. A can of tomato soup. Now let's get down to business."

"Bernie! Why'd you have to spoil it?" Mom protested, as Lolly made a face and said, "Tomato soup?"

"Tomato soup." Mom looked pleased with herself. "No one would ever suspect."

"Eddie." Pop turned to me. "Come on, now. Let's lay it all out on the table and see where we're at. It's time to solve this thing."

"Wait a minute," Mom said, pushing her chair back from the table. "My knee is bothering me again. I have to put it up on something." She put her left leg up on the seat of the adjoining chair. "Eddie, could you ask them to bring me some chopped ice in a dish towel?"

"I'll ask Erma to bring you a regular ice pack." I went over to the intercom on the wall, rang housekeeping, and put in the request.

"Is it from all that folk dancing?" I asked Mom, concerned about the way she was rubbing her knee and wincing.

"I think maybe I overdid the overdoing," Mom said. "A steel knee, believe it or not, is not as strong as a real knee, and it doesn't work as well."

"Maybe you should give up the folk dancing," Lolly suggested.

Mom looked horrified at the thought, and spent the next few minutes telling Lolly, and the rest of us, exactly why she felt that it was important that she keep up her dancing.

Finally, Erma appeared with the ice pack, cutting her short.

As soon as the housekeeper had left the room again, Pop said, "*Now* can we get to work?" He sounded at the limit of his patience with a frivolous world of mixed-up priorities. "You want me to figure out who did it, or don't you?"

"I want anyone here to figure out who did it," I said. "It's gotten to the point where this case is on my mind almost all the time. Pretty soon, it's going to start interfering with what the taxpayers are paying me for."

"No problem," Pop said in his just-leave-everything-to-me tone. "I'll solve the crime for you right now, Eddie."

"How are you going to do that?" If only it could somehow be as easy as Pop made it sound.

"First, brief me. I know you talked to all the suspects twice and the second time around they lied to you a little bit less than the first time. So bring me up to date on what you found out when I wasn't around."

"You were there at the second round with Beverly Benson and Ken Lang, so you don't need that, but Lolly does, so why don't we start with that. You brief Lolly and then she'll brief you on Gur, the Mardins, and Donna Krieg. I'm trying to remember something, and maybe it'll come to me if I keep quiet a little longer."

"What are you trying to remember?" Lolly asked.

I gave her a look. "If I *knew,* I wouldn't be trying to remember it, would I?"

"So think," Pop told me, and addressed Lolly. "Meanwhile, I'll fill you in. To begin with, Mrs. Benson cut off the end of the phone tape, in which she threatened to cut Krieg's heart out. Then she forgot to tell you about how when Krieg and his wife came in, he told her to forget about Monday, when he had promised to pay her the two million he owed her."

"Oh. It doesn't sound good," Lolly admitted. "But that doesn't mean she killed him. I've said worse things about the telephone company."

"If we were sure who the killer is," I interrupted my thinking to say, "we wouldn't be sitting around here trying to find who the killer is. All Pop is doing is reporting. File it in your think tank." I turned to my father. "Tell Lolly about Ken Lang."

"This one is simple. Ken Lang didn't get cheated out of three hundred thousand by Karl Krieg, he got cheated out of six hundred thousand. An accountant yet. And his wife doesn't know. So when he said he was going to kill Krieg, there was twice the reason for him to do it, plus the reason that Krieg was going to blackmail him in addition, by threatening to tell Lang's wife."

"Pardon my language," Lolly said to my mother before turning back to Pop and announcing, "that bastard deserved to die."

"But not at Bevvy's wedding," I put in, "and the Langs', too."

"Under the circumstances any of them found themselves in," Lolly said, "I would have killed him myself."

"But in a smarter way," Pop said, then asked me, "any luck?"

"No. There's something I need to remember, but it just won't come to me. It's driving me nuts."

"Can I say something?" Mom asked, clutching the ice pack against her knee.

"Sure." I expected her to change the subject back to folk dancing or chocolate cake, but she didn't. To my surprise, she made an observation about the Krieg case.

"From what I've been hearing," she said, "and with you smart people breaking your heads for a week, even more than a week, it looks to me like the murder was accomplished in the most intelligent way possible. So maybe if you just picked the smartest person, he'd be the one. Or she."

I looked at Lolly. "Maybe Mom has the key. Pick the smartest one and concentrate on him. Or her."

"The trouble is," Lolly said, "that they're all very smart."

"Except Donna Krieg," I said.

"Wrong," Lolly said. "She may be the smartest of them all. Big boobs do not a moron make, and you don't learn intelligence in school. If you consider where and what she probably came from and how she survived, think about how you would have lived, how you would have managed, if at all, under those conditions. And when you consider how rich she'll be when she figures out how to find where her husband's stashed his money—and she probably will—be a little respectful, too."

"So you're saying Donna's still a prime suspect?" I asked. I still wasn't so sure.

"One of the primest," Lolly said firmly. "Now I'll continue to bring your father up to date. Ed and I interviewed Moshe Gur. Ed said that Gur always told the literal truth, and after talking with him, I believe that, though I could be wrong. Ed figured out that Krieg had flashed his blackmail envelope at Gur, the one that was full of cut paper and looked like it held a lot of money. Krieg threatened to have it found where it would be clear that Gur had accepted it as a bribe. Gur swore he didn't murder Krieg because it's against the Torah."

"That happens to be true," Pop said.

"I know," Lolly told him, "but Ed deliberately didn't ask Gur if he killed Krieg."

"You missed a good opportunity to clear things up," Pop said. "Even if he was innocent, you would've had one less prime suspect."

"And one less of my best commissioners," I explained. "I can always ask him, if I have to." Back to Lolly. "Our visit to the Mardins?"

"Frank and Joan Mardin own the Jomar Development Corporation," Lolly said, "a large construction company that is down to skin and bones and will soon be bankrupt. They're using the last of their capital to stay afloat until the Muni Yard job is awarded, but they had no hope of being selected while Karl Krieg had the use of Beverly Benson's firm and expertise. They believe, probably rightly, that with Krieg dead, Beverly, with whom they've worked before, will tie up with them under reasonable conditions and that this will ensure their designation as developers of the project. This will raise them from poverty to riches almost instantly and allow them to function as developers again, to do work they love. At their age, it's almost certainly the last sizable project they will ever do. They had a very strong motive to kill Karl Krieg."

"Do you want me to tell about Donna Krieg?" I asked.

"Your unbiased view?" Lolly asked. "Or do you still have a red dress floating before your eyes?"

"Oh, please. You want to tell it? Go ahead."

Lolly did. "Donna lied about almost everything she told us at the first interview. She's considerably older than everyone thinks, and she didn't quite have the job history she claims. She didn't marry for love; she married Karl Krieg because she thought she could make a lot of money with him and because he was twenty years older and lived an unhealthy life. I think she was telling the truth when she said he stole her money, that he didn't trust her with money, that he made his money by cheating, that he used her in his high-finance con games, that he kept her almost as a slave, and that he cheated on her regularly."

"That last part is definitely true," I put in. "Everyone in New York knows about Karl Krieg's bimbos."

"Exactly," Lolly said. "Anyway, he hid his money where she couldn't find it and, though she's far from poverty-stricken with saved money she hid from him, she doesn't have enough money to invest in anything that will support her without working. She had an excellent motive for killing him."

"So you've still got five prime suspects," Pop said.

"But we know a good deal more about them," I said.

"Okay, so all of them had good strong motives, strong enough to kill for," Pop said. "What about opportunities?"

"In a sense, they all had good opportunities," I said. "The whole murder took a few seconds, two, three, four, five, we don't know how many, exactly, but every one of the suspects was within a few feet of the alcove where the murder took place within the window of opportunity, which was no more than ten minutes long."

"What about the wedding pictures?" Lolly asked suddenly. "You looked at them, Ed. What did you find?"

"I have over a hundred pictures, and each of the suspects appears in several shots. The trouble is, not only don't we know the exact time the murder was committed, but we don't know the exact time each picture was taken. Wherever the suspect was when the picture was taken, a few seconds later he was somewhere else, guaranteed."

"What about the means?" Pop asked. "You know—means, motive, and opportunity."

"How do you know all this?" I asked.

"You think I do nothing but play pinochle?" Pop said. "First of all, I listened when I was at the Merkin. There are plenty of cops in this city who appreciate perfect hand-sliced pastrami—"

"I know, you told me," I cut in, trying to waylay him before he got started on that track.

For a change, the diversion worked.

"Second of all," Pop continued, "I read. You know, you can learn a lot just from reading."

Where had I heard that before?

"And last, I not only read the New York papers, I watch television, too. So why are you surprised that I know what's what? You think you inherited your brains only from your mother?"

"Of course not."

"So tell me about the murder weapon."

"I already told you." Silence. "Okay, I'll tell you again. A very slim blade, maybe eight inches long and three-quarters of an inch wide, with a sharp point and a slight curve at the pointed end. All edges razor-sharp, with a square end opposite the point."

"No handle, right?"

"Some paper napkins wrapped around the end."

"Did you ever see such a thing in your life, Eddie?"

"No, and I never heard of it, either, not even when I was a lawyer."

"So why should it be such a funny shape?"

"Well, it was perfect for stabbing Krieg."

"Underhand, right? With the left hand?"

"Had to be, from the position of the body."

"Okay, which one of the suspects is left-handed?"

"None of them," I said, having previously considered this point and checked my notes.

"Well, are any of them ambi . . . what do you call it?"

"Ambidextrous? I have no idea, Pop, but I imagine the police have checked that out already."

"Just for good measure, did you check out what they checked out? You can never be too sure."

"I'm tired," Mom said abruptly, "and this conversation is getting you nowhere. Mind if I go watch some television in our room?"

"You need my help?" Pop asked her as she shifted in her seat and braced her hands on the table.

"I can manage. I'll take the ice bag for good luck."

She got up and limped out of the room, waving and calling good night over her shoulder.

I frowned, watching her absently as the thought I had been trying to grab for days danced tantalizingly close, then flitted away again.

"We're going around in circles," Lolly said after Mom had gone. "Missing something. Maybe we should all call it a day."

"I guess you're right," Pop said. "I'll go join Lillian. Maybe something will come to me while I'm sleeping."

"I think I'll leave, too," Lolly said.

"I'll take you home," I offered.

"That's okay," she said. "Stay with your folks; I'll call for a taxi."

"Are you sure?"

"I'm positive." Lolly stood up and yawned. "Sweet dreams, everyone."

To be honest, I didn't mind not seeing her home. I was really pooped and I decided to go to bed early.

Who knew, something might come to me while I slept.

Nothing came to me while I slept; it came in those two seconds between sleeping and waking up. Complete. All in two seconds.

I knew who had murdered Karl Krieg.

I knew why.

I knew how.

I also knew it was useless . . . there was no way to prove anything.

Eleven days of working my brains to the bone, and Lolly's and Pop's brains, too, and there was no way to bring the killer to justice.

At least, I hadn't thought of a way just yet.

But I would.

I had to.

_____TWENTY

On the way to City Hall the next morning, I kept my eyes closed, which I rarely do.

For once, I didn't want to see what was going on in the streets of my beloved city; I just wanted to focus, without distractions, on how to catch a killer when there was no proof.

Riding down Seventh Avenue with my eyes closed didn't tell me anything about the murder case, but it told me something I had never known about myself. Closing my eyes in a moving car when I've got nothing more than coffee and grapefruit juice in my stomach makes me queasy.

So, by the time we reached midtown, I had no choice but to look out the windows. It was either that, or make conversation with Ben Krim, who was sitting beside me, guarding my body.

They don't call Seventh Avenue "Fashion Avenue" for nothing. I watched one well-dressed pedestrian after another hurrying along the sidewalk on the way to work. Most of the biggest designers in the world have showrooms in this neighborhood, and the people who work in them tend to look like they just stepped out of *Vogue.*

We stopped at the light at the intersection of Thirty-fourth Street, in front of Macy's, and my gaze rested absently on a tall, gorgeous dark-skinned woman who was waiting to cross. She was wearing a turban on her head, and her lanky body was clad in some kind of slinky black tights under a long, sweeping black coat. Under her arm, she clutched a narrow, rectangular purse.

I tore my thoughts away from the Krieg murder when I noticed a shady-looking man in slouchy clothes and a baseball cap sidling up next to the woman on the curb, eyeing her bag.

Why, I wondered, wasn't she carrying one of those enormous carryalls that most women in this city seem to favor? Not only do oversize bags allow them to carry anything and everything, but they obviously thwart purse snatchers.

I was about to roll down my window and shout a warning to the woman on the corner when the Walk sign appeared and she started across the avenue in front of us, hugging her bag under her arm and giving the would-be thief a nasty look over her shoulder, as if she had known he was there all along.

The light changed again, and the limo started moving forward.

I frowned and glanced back over my shoulder.

The woman in black had disappeared into the crowd.

But I had an idea. Not a surefire idea, but the best I could come up with, one that might work.

In my office, I asked Rosemary to stall my early meeting with Claudia Morgan, who heads the city's Human Resources Administration. I hated to do it, since my responsibilities as mayor should always come first. But then again, I reasoned that bringing Karl Krieg's killer to justice *was* city business, since doing so would clear my name and the names of some of New York's most prominent citizens.

I sat in my leather chair and started going through the wedding pictures that Don O'Sullivan had given me. I already knew what I was going to find, but I had to make sure.

I flipped past shots of the bride and groom alone, and concentrated on the candids of the guests. Within minutes, I had my proof. Three of the photos clearly showed what I remembered.

I went over to my desk and buzzed Rosemary. "Can you stall Claudia a few minutes more?"

"She's not going to be thrilled. You know she's not a morning person in the first place."

I rolled my eyes. The woman was grumpy any time of day, and Rosemary knew it.

"I need more time," I said. "Tell her I'm in the middle of an unexpected crisis, and that I'll be with her as soon as possible."

"What's the crisis?"

"You'll find out soon enough."

Rosemary sighed. "Fine. I'll stall her."

I pulled out my notebook that contained information on all of the suspects, and got busy.

I invited each of them to dine with me tonight at Gracie Mansion. And I made sure that they all knew it was not just a social invitation.

Moshe and Ruth Gur took some extra persuading, since today was Friday, the Sabbath. I promised them that everything—the food, silver, dishes—would be *glatt* kosher, meaning absolutely positively kosher according to religious law.

My next call was to Hinda Grisin of Fab Affairs.

"Mr. Mayor," she said, sounding surprised—and more than a little wary. "I had hoped I'd hear from you again. I didn't think it would be so soon, though."

"I need an enormous favor from you."

"If it's about that murder, I already told you—"

"It is related to the murder, but what I need from you is strictly professional."

"What is it?"

"A fabulous *glatt* kosher meal for fourteen, including sweet sacramental wines."

There was a pause. "When did you need it?"

"Tonight. At Gracie Mansion."

"I see. Don't you have a personal chef?"

"I do, but Lucien is off this Friday. Listen, I know it's short notice, but I really hope you can help me, Hinda."

"I'll be glad to," she said after another long pause.

I sighed in relief. "I appreciate it. Now, if possible, the help should include some of the people who worked at the wedding in the chapel. The bill for everything will go to me personally."

"Do you have anything in particular in mind for the menu?"

"As a matter of fact, I do. I want heavy, sense-dulling foods served and the wine to flow like water."

"I think that can be arranged."

"Good."

I needed every little advantage I could get.

My final call was to Charley Deacon. I invited him to dinner. At first, he hemmed and hawed.

"Ed, I'm really busy working on the case. Since this whole thing began, I haven't had a good night's sleep or a decent meal—"

"All the more reason for you to come to dinner. I'm having it catered."

"But the case is—"

"Charley, listen. This has something to do with the case. I'll explain it to you later, before the other guests arrive. If you come to dinner, I can almost guarantee you that you'll arrest the killer before the night is over."

I hoped.

If all went well and the gods were smiling.

Mom and Pop were seated near the end of the table to my left, with Lolly between them and me. Moshe and Ruth Gur were to my right. Charley Deacon, who had been fully briefed on my plan, was at the end of the table to my right, and Donna Krieg sat at the other end. Across the table from me, May and Ken Lang were at the left, Joan and Frank Mardin in the middle, and Beverly and Ralph Benson were to my right.

Not the best arrangement for light conversation, but this was not a party.

If my deduction was correct, one of the guests gathered at the table was a cold-blooded killer.

Apparently, I wasn't the only one who was aware of that fact. Conversation had been strained, to say the least, throughout the main courses.

I made sure decaffeinated coffee was served with dessert—no stimulants for my prime suspects. Finally, when the noodle pudding dishes had been removed, I rang a glass with my knife and spoke.

"As is obvious to all of you, this is not just a friendly dinner. I now know who the killer is and how the murder was done. While you're all good people, I am obligated to reveal what I know and turn the killer over to the proper authorities in the person of Detective Sergeant Charles Deacon, at the end of the table."

"So reveal already," Ralph Benson said. "Let's be done with this whole affair."

"Not yet," I said. "I have to put everything in perspective. First, Ken Lang."

He clutched his wife's hand and started to turn blue. "No details will be discussed," I said hastily, and Ken started breathing again.

"Karl Krieg cheated him out of a large amount of money. Like all of you, Mr. Lang was seen by everyone near the alcove where Krieg was found and was not seen for several minutes during the time of the murder."

"Next," I said, nodding in Bevvy's direction, "Mrs. Benson. She was cheated out of an even larger sum of money and, additionally, was threatened by Krieg that he would frame her on a charge of which she was innocent."

Bevvy reached for her nearly empty wineglass and drained it in one long gulp.

"Moshe Gur," I went on, "was threatened with being framed if he didn't facilitate Krieg's winning the Muni Yard Project."

Moshe and Ruth clasped hands on the table, both wearing solemn expressions.

"The Mardins are close to bankruptcy, losing everything they worked for all their lives, due to Krieg's machinations."

Joan and Frank exchanged a glance, then faced me again, almost looking defiant.

"And Donna Krieg," I concluded, "was lied to, cheated, and treated like a slave by her deceased husband."

The widow, who tonight was wearing a black crepe dress and a somber expression, lowered her gaze to the ivory linen tablecloth.

The only sound in the room was the ticking of the clock on the mantel. I allowed a full minute to go by before I continued.

"So what we have is a group of people, all of whom had the motive and the opportunity to kill Karl Krieg. We have the means too; a piece of flat steel, an eighth-inch-thick, three-quarters of an inch wide and eight inches long, with a slight curve at one end, pointed and sharpened at the sides and point.''

I paused momentarily to let that sink in, and wondered what the killer was thinking.

"The one thing we don't have is how the knife was smuggled into the chapel. The knife was clearly made for the purpose of killing Krieg and a handle was made by wrapping several napkins around the square end of the blade. Why not a regular handle? And why at the chapel rather than the Plaza?''

I turned to Donna. "Karl was not in good physical condition, was he?''

"The only reason he didn't beat me," Donna said, "was that the first time he ever slapped me, I bounced him on his fat head using one hand.''

"So if he had his back in a corner of the alcove, anyone could come in and, hidden by the curtains, put a hand on his head to hold it in place and slip the knife into his heart with the other hand.''

At her end of the table, my mother gave a little groan and closed her eyes briefly, looking pale. No one else looked fazed by the gory details, including the killer.

"From the location of the body," I said, "it would have been the right hand that was raised to the victim's head, with the left holding the knife.''

"Considering Karl's physical condition, a twelve-year-old girl could do that," Donna pointed out. "It wouldn't even need to be someone my size.''

"Exactly," I agreed, and went on to the next point. "So why the chapel and not the Plaza? First, there are people coming and going all the time in the Plaza. No real privacy and someone could walk in on you any second. In the chapel, all the murderer had to do was whisper something to Krieg, tell him you had to see him alone for a moment, and follow him into the alcove.''

I let my gaze rove around the table, resting on one suspect after another, and finally on Charley Deacon, who appeared poised and ready.

"So the question boils down to how the knife was brought into the chapel. Whoever brought it in, killed Karl Krieg. And I know the answer.''

Silence.

It was as if all of them, innocent and guilty alike, were afraid to breathe, afraid to make the slightest move, and risk incrimination.

"How the knife was brought in is amazingly simple. All the women were carrying evening bags of various kinds, handles and clutches, side-snap closures, split-snap, and combinations and variations of these. When guests came to the metal detector, the men had to empty their pockets into little baskets and walk through. The women had to put their evening bags into the basket before walking through. Anything closed, such as the bags, was opened and checked by the police officer in charge to ensure that nothing was in the bag that shouldn't be there. But they didn't examine the frame of the bag. The frame holding the top snap held the murder weapon, which is why the knife had to be flat and thin.''

Now I was speaking directly to Charley Deacon, who looked duly impressed, even though he'd heard this all when I'd briefed him earlier.

"My memory is very good, but for this I checked the wedding photographs. Only one prime suspect had a bag that fit that description." I paused dramatically, then, at Charley's slight nod, played my ace. "That suspect is Mrs. Joan Mardin.''

A collective sigh of relief went around the table like a wave.

Joan jumped up and shouted wildly, "I didn't! This is crazy, Ed. I swear I didn't do it! I already told you why killing him wouldn't help." She began crying, huge, gasping sobs. "Tell them, Frank. Tell them I didn't do it.''

Frank's eyes looked glazed, and he didn't flinch as his wife clutched at his sleeve.

Charley Deacon had quietly moved up behind Joan Mardin. "I'll have to ask you to come with me," he said. "Please put your hands behind your back." He took out his handcuffs.

Joan let out a high-pitched wail. "No! I'm innocent,'' she sobbed hysterically. "Frank, please, make them stop!''

At last, Frank Mardin sprang to life.

"Don't touch her," he told Deacon, reaching out to stop the

detective before he could slap the cuffs on his wife. "She's telling the truth. She didn't do it."

"Please sit down, sir," Charley said calmly. "I appreciate how you feel, but I have to take her in for questioning." To Joan, he said, again, "I'm asking you politely, madam, please put your hands behind your back. Please don't make me call for my men."

"Don't touch her," Frank said. "She didn't do it." He paused and flinched, then swallowed hard.

Under the table, I clenched my hands in my lap, waiting to see if my plan had worked.

"I know she didn't do it," Frank Mardin announced in a defeated tone, "because I did."

I let out the breath I hadn't even known I'd been holding, a long, satisfying sigh of relief that my plan had worked.

There was stunned silence for only another split second, then a murmur went up among the guests around the table, and above it, Joan Mardin screamed again. This time, she protested, "No! Not you, Frank. Tell me it wasn't you!"

Charley let go of her and pulled her husband up out of his seat, not roughly, but firmly, and slapped the cuffs on his hands in one easy movement.

As soon as Joan saw what had happened, she lunged at Charley. Before she could touch him, Ken Lang and Ralph Benson had grabbed her and subdued her. She slumped into a chair, weeping quietly.

"How did you do it, Frank?" Charley asked. "You might as well tell us."

But Mardin looked too overcome to speak. He was trembling all over, and his jaw had gone slack.

"I'll tell you, and everyone else, how he did it," I volunteered, when Mardin wouldn't speak. At last, I had the opportunity to reveal the key to the case—the revelation that had come to me early this morning, thanks to Mom.

"Frank told me," I began, "that a few years back, because of arthritis, he'd had a hip prosthesis put in. Steel and plastic. Whenever he has to go through a metal detector, he would have to tell the security person, so that he could bypass the detector. The security person would then go over him with a hand-held sensor."

I paused and locked my eyes on Frank Mardin's.

"He made a flat blade in the shop—he would have plenty of idle time now that business has slumped. It was the size and shape of the hip prosthesis, and he taped it in the right place with a little gauze over it. The detector wouldn't be able to tell it from the hip prosthesis. Once he got inside the chapel, he went to the bathroom and put the knife into his pocket. Isn't that right, Frank?"

At last, Mardin lifted his head and nodded. He turned to Joan, who was now weeping quietly, and said in a raw voice, "It's all right, dear. I couldn't let them hurt you."

The door to the dining room opened, and several NYPD detectives Charley had posted there entered the room. Within moments, they were leading the handcuffed Frank out.

Charley stayed behind and told Joan that he would accompany her to the station so that she could be there when they booked Frank.

As he helped her to her feet, Joan turned to me. "Why did you do it, Ed? You knew how Frank and I felt about each other. You knew he would never let me be falsely accused. You used the way he feels about me to make him confess."

"You're absolutely right," I agreed, "and I have no regrets. I did it because it's my job and my duty."

"But Karl Krieg was a bastard, Ed. You know it. Everyone in this room knows it."

"You can't go around murdering people, not even if they're bad guys," I said simply. "Now stop crying and listen to me."

"But—"

"Stop, Mrs. Mardin. If you want to help your husband, stop." She almost stopped. Good enough. "Get yourself a good criminal attorney. There are dozens in New York. I have a list of some of them here." I took a folded sheet from my breast pocket and passed it to her.

"I can't afford one," she said limply, but she clutched the paper in her fist.

"You might be able to."

"But how . . . ?"

"It was clear when we visited you that you were running the company and Frank was doing the engineering and architecture.

Assuming Frank can't get out on bail while the DA is making up his mind, you can hire or retain architects and engineers. Now, where do we get the money you need?" I looked at Beverly Benson. "Would you take on Jomar Development for the Muni Yard Project?"

Bevvy, who had looked positively glib ever since she herself had been exonerated, said, "I would if I saw a way for them to pay me."

"You will," I assured her, and looked at Moshe Gur. "Any objection to considering Jomar for the project?"

He thought carefully and said, "If an officer or stockholder of the company is not under indictment for a crime, I have no problem."

Back to Joan. "Have Frank sign over all stock to you irrevocably. Use the same lawyer."

Lang coughed. "You'll be all right too," I said. I looked at Bevvy. "And you too."

"Am I the only one who's not going to be all right?" Donna asked.

"Of course not," I said, taking two sets of papers out of my magic pocket and putting them on the table. "Sign all of these."

She left them on the table and asked suspiciously, "What are they?"

"They're promissory notes to pay Mr. Lang and Mrs. Benson the money your husband cheated them out of, plus interest, first, before you get the rest of the money, when you find the money your husband hid away."

"I don't even know how much money it is," Donna said. "I could end up with nothing."

I turned to Lolly, who had been waiting patiently all this time. "Tell her."

"Gladly." Lolly addressed Donna. "In raising money from investors, it's a common practice for the active partner to deposit show money, earnest money, as a symbol of good faith and to prove he has the ability to pay for the initial fringe expenses. It's usually one percent of the total venture. Since this is a four-billion-dollar project, it has to be forty million dollars."

"And how much are Lang and Benson owed?" Donna asked.

Ken turned blue again.

I said, "Lang is well under a million and Benson is about two and a quarter million."

"I'll sign," Donna said, "but I'm adding that I have to end up with at least twenty million."

"Reasonable," I said. "And now I have a business proposition to suggest. Donna, invest half the money you end up with in Jomar Development. Look into it yourself, but I believe it'll be a highly profitable investment. Now, Lolly, I have another question. Krieg has to have some fancy money right here in New York. How much?"

"From what I can deduce," she said, "about a quarter million. But there's no way to get it; it's under a code name."

"And where is the forty million?"

"That's easy; in a Singapore bank. But again, I don't know in what name."

"If I give you the name, can your people find it? The New York money, too?"

"With a name? At the speed of light."

I rose and looked around the room, feeling mighty pleased with myself.

"What does Krieg mean?" I asked. "In German?"

"War," Pop answered promptly.

"So how about Warbucks," I said, "like the cartoon character?"

"That's it!" Donna said excitedly. "It has to be. 'Little Orphan Annie' was Karl's favorite comic strip."

I shrugged and fought the urge to take a bow.

Lolly looked at me. "You're a genius, Ed. Do you know that?"

"Of course I know that. Why do you think I'm the mayor?"